PRAISE FOR

BY DAVID TROMBLAY

"David Tromblay has created a violent and wistful elegy to small-town America that cuts as sharp as an ice pick and goes twice as deep."
—S.A. Cosby, author of ***Blacktop Wasteland***

"Tromblay is a natural storyteller with an ear tuned for dialogue and an imagination that will keep readers wide-eyed and guessing, slack-jawed, and entertained. A manhunt shouldn't be this fun."
—David Joy, author of ***When These Mountains Burn***

"***Sangre Road*** is spectacular! From slow-burn to inferno in character development, story and inventive twists and unexpected turns."
—Stephen Mack Jones, author of ***August Snow*** and ***Dead of Winter***

"Quick-witted, fast-paced, unpredictable. All roads converge to make ***Sangre Road*** a raucous, wide-open, crime-riddled joy ride."
—Michael Farris Smith, author of ***Nick*** and ***Blackwood***

"***Sangre Road*** is a wild trip through a surreal Clinton-era Oklahoma, paced like a small-town stock car race without any rules. And funny as hell to boot."
—Scott Phillips, author of ***That Left Turn at Albuquerque*** and T*he Ice Harvest*

"***Sangre Road*** is a gritty, funny crime caper that beats with a big heart. It's one part Coen Brothers, one part Elmore Leonard, but also a beast all its own. It takes you to unexpected places and leaves you thinking."
—Nick Kolakowski, author of ***Boise Longpig Hunting Club*** and ***A Brutal Bunch of Heartbroken Saps***

"Tromblay's writing is easy to fall into because he is clear and funny, and just when you're relaxed, he'll hit you with a line that makes you go 'hell yeah.' ***Sangre Road*** is alive with the weirdo types of characters you'd see on a given day in Oklahoma, and their color and humanity shine through. Truly a pleasure to read crime fiction this good."
—J. David Osborne, author of ***Black Gum***

More Praise for Sangre Road

"A rough-and-tumble journey through a landscape as colorful as its inhabitants."

—Steph Post, author of *Lightwood*

"David Tromblay has done that thing we don't get enough of; a remarkably unlikeable character dropped into a book that'll make you turn the pages regardless. Tone, smell, dust, and heat all live here on **Sangre Road**, and the chop-along dialogue will speed you right down to the end of the trail. Buckle up!"

—Theo Van Alst Jr, author of *Sacred Smokes*

"David Tromblay's **Sangre Road** pulsates with intensity. It's scrappy, sharp-edged, wild, and funny. One hell of a memorable ride."

—William Boyle, author of *City of Margins* and *Gravesend*

"A thrill ride through Oklahoma alongside the stubborn, punch-drunk, smart-mouthed bounty hunter Moses Kincaid, complete with bikers, prison peckerwoods, zombies, pro midget wrestlers, no-tell motels, greasy-spoon diners, and enough mouthfuls of heavy-duty pain pills to keep you asking, 'what's next?'"

—Penni Jones, author of *Suicide Souls* and *On the Bricks*

OTHER TITLES BY **DAVID TROMBLAY**

As You Were: A Memoir
The Essentials: A Manifesto
The Rambling of the Revenant

David Tromblay

Sangre Road

SHOTGUN
HONEY
2 0 2 1

Published by Shotgun Honey, an imprint of Down & Out Books.

Shotgun Honey
215 Loma Road
Charleston, WV 25314
www.ShotgunHoney.com

Down & Out Books
3959 Van Dyke Rd, Ste. 265
Lutz, FL 33558
www.DownAndOutBooks.com

Cover Design by Bad Fido.

First Printing 2021.

ISBN-10: 1-64396-191-8
ISBN-13: 978-1-64396-191-0

For my daughter, Dalia,
who slept the summer mornings away
while I wrote this all down.
Fly high, baby girl,
and rest in peace.

Sangre Road

1

THE RED DIRT CHOP SHOP has a 1968 Chevy Custom Camper sans camper for sale down on the tail end of Sangre Road. How much they want for it is soaped on the windshield but blocked by a sign that cannot be read so well. It's gone into disrepair—the sign, not the truck—like a family plot with no more relations above ground. The sign is sort of impaled on a four-by-four-inch post somebody whittled down until it got small enough that all four of the set screws could be tightened. I know this because I wanted to know how much they wanted for the truck, and, then, since I was idling on the shoulder of said Sangre Road, I took however long to look over the cast-iron historical marker which read:

> *THE LAST "BOOMER" TOWN*
> *About ¾ mi. east of here*

> *300 armed "boomers" made their last stand for settlement of Oklahoma country, led by Wm. V. Courtright, and surrendered to U.S. Calvary troops commanded by Col. J. Hastings, Jan. 26,*

1885. On this site, the "boomers" built log cabins and dugouts for their town of Lawson, founded on Dec. 12, 1884.

Seeing how the town was established and surrendered in the span of six weeks and the sight itself is now nothing more than a few acres of decrepit automobiles, it all seemed insignificant and extraneous—not warranting the casting of a marker. There wasn't even one of the brown signs telling motorists a historical marker waited up ahead.

Saying *surrendered* seems like it wasn't all that bloody of a battle, being there was no mention of a body count on the marker, but there is the matter of their naming the road *Sangre*, meaning: *blood* en español. Figuring in how the Spanish-speaking population here is nada, I'd wager it's a roundabout way of them covering up a bloody past but kinda-sorta acknowledging it without outright saying the boogeyman's name.

$3,000 firm was the price on the Chevy. It comes with a spiderwebbed windshield, no bumpers, and every inch of it is primered black, which makes me think it's either dinged to hell or comes with a full rust package.

No thank you.

This way of thinking is what you get when you spend too much time by yourself alone in an automobile. But I wouldn't have to stay inside my head a whole lot longer, luckily. Sangre Road became a smorgasbord of signs and ads once I crept inside the city limits.

A diner stood right on the other side of the fifth church I passed, the one with the marquee that read: *No one is perfect, Moses was once a basket case.*

I ordered a sweet tea as a show of faith to let them

know I meant to differentiate myself as a customer rather than a loitering member of the public, then I made my hurried pilgrimage to the men's room.

After taking a swig of their world-famous sweet tea, in walked a man boasting all the physical attributes of a double-sized soft-serve ice cream cone, the extra creamy kind made with double the milk fat. Prescription glasses with lenses tinted the color of watered-down rosé wine clung to the tip of his nose. I say prescription because when he tilted his head back to find an open table, he became bug-eyed.

His dress shirt was one with ruffles sewn into the chest, though it wasn't the bleached white you'd see someone wear with an older tuxedo. I imagine it was sold as ivory, but it was the color of a midmorning piss following the downing of an entire pot of coffee along with some multivitamin with 1000% of the recommended daily values.

Both pockets on the chest of that shirt were packed with pens, sans pocket protectors. He was obviously a man who liked to live dangerously. He'd filled the left side with what I'll call Easter or pastel colors, while the right side was all primary pen ink colors: black, blue, red, and two others: one looked to be stainless steel, and the other was a gold-plated pen. Both of which could have held any imaginable color of ink.

Around his neck hung a shoelace, weighed down with no less than two dozen keys—by my count. A fist sat plopped atop a cane in which he lent far too much trust. I only say so because of how the floor let out a muffled cry, announcing his presence a few short seconds before each footfall. Other folks passed through the dining area without the floorboards offering a word of protest. It could have been the light playing with the lacquer, but I'd swear I saw that cane bow each time he hobbled this way and that. He'd swayed through the side door, too, which was a little wider than the front door—to allow for deliveries—and led straight into the kitchen. His pendulum gait hypnotized me; I am embarrassed to admit. That's how the waitress surprised me and announced her presence by setting down the sweating glass of ice water as she asked me, "Are you ready to order, or are you going to need another minute with the menu?"

"Yes, I am," I said with an embarrassed smile, "I am indeed going to need a few more minutes, please. Everything sounds so mouth-wateringly delicious."

I went with a pecan waffle and what they called Huevos Mexicano. The latter came with hash browns and toast and jelly or biscuits and gravy. I went with the latter coupling thinking the gravy would add a little sustenance to the meal. Without the drink, it came to ten bucks. Not too bad. The trip to the bathroom did not lead me to believe the meal should come with a complimentary tetanus shot, so I found myself in better spirits than when I realized where this latest paper trail had brought me.

The telephone book I acquired from the phone booth outside of the Get-N-Go was no thicker than a weekly edition of the TV Guide. From that alone, I knew I'd be on my way in no time at all—and cue the Caruso of Rock to remind me of the day they hung my name in the fool's hall of fame.

Bolstered by the aforementioned short-sighted assurance of the ease of how fast I'd be pulling a U-turn, I got a motel room. I took advantage of their hourly rates where it's well known no one wants to be seen or see who is coming and going, where I could shit, shower, shave, and get to work—without being bothered about when I was checking out.

I may have never visited this town before, but I knew the place well enough. The public library operates on banker's hours, there are as many adult bookstores as churches, and you cannot, no way, no how, buy a beer on the Lord's day.

Atop that, sat the conundrum of living in a city so small is that every citizen shoulders the stress of celebrity. That's to say when everyone is bored, nobody else is boring. There's no minding your own business. Everyone is family. Not necessarily blood, but there's a closeness that causes me claustrophobia.

Being so fresh a face in so small a town, I knew I couldn't set up somewhere and surveil someone without more eyes looking my way than what would have proved beneficial. It's like that adage warning away from pointing a finger at someone because there'll be three others pointing back at your own self.

I borrowed the bible from the bedside table the Gideons placed in my room and stood out on the corner closest to the Jefferson Lines station and preached the Word to passing cars.

Silly as it may seem, it's the perfect platform to watch the comings and goings and not have to worry about being an unfamiliar face and drawing too much attention to my own self.

I call it tradecraft.

A curbside crazy is easy enough to ignore and hiding in plain sight is a whole lot less nerve-racking when you're a stranger in a strange land and do not know who it is you need to watch out for other than who you came to find. In that same breath, a panhandler holding a sign and begging for whatever change you can spare may draw the attention of the authorities depending on local ordinances, but not a sidewalk preacher. Especially in a place where everyone is so afraid of coming off as a piss-poor Christian. I make such speculation about my new-found workplace based upon seeing so many bumper stickers mentioning Him that you'd swear He was up for reelection.

If ever I'd take note of someone taking too much stock in what I was saying or doing or where I was loitering, I could always cook up a splash of misdirection.

The first instance I felt compelled to do so during this job was with a gentleman who came out of the hospi-tal in a wheelchair looking like he was still getting the mechanics of it down, and, poor him, he hadn't anyone to give him a push. Though he wheeled his own self into the package store with enough ease.

When he exited and came across the intersection toward me, I did not hesitate to seize such an opportune moment and did what I could to divert the attention of every driver toward him. By God, by some miracle, he was able to stand and walk and navigate that wheel-chair up and over the median without dumping the case of beer or any of the bottles of liquor hidden away in the brown paper sacks, which were now riding in the wheelchair. It was quite a sight. I did not want a single soul to miss it, so I hollered out, proclaimed, "It's a mir-acle, right before our very eyes, brothers and sisters! Just hearing the Lord's message has helped this man to walk again. Rise and walk! Rise and walk, my son!" I screamed above the knocking engines and the nauseating exhaust tightening my chest. "Rise and walk. You don't need no wheelchair. Go on and tell your doctor how he has failed you, but it is the Lord who has healed you."

If only there were cameras around to capture the moment.

I'd bet my trigger finger he was hoping against all hope there wasn't anyone from the insurance company within earshot, too.

He put his head down once he saw how he was being followed and judged by every eyeball inside every stopped vehicle.

One searing gaze was cause enough for him to lift his heels a touch higher than normal and get as far from me as fast as his feet could carry him—and there were at least a dozen and a half staring him down.

Amen for that.

If any of those glances drifted over to me in his absence, I'd toss around words like *judgment* and *abomination* and *His return* until every last set of eyeballs fixated on the dangling traffic lights. Doing so got each car to creep toward the intersection in a clear demonstration of their building impatience and want over need for the light to go from red to green.

2

ERIC DRUMGOOLE SCRAMBLED out of town hours before a scheduled court appearance, which meant he skipped out on a bond worth more than his house, car, as well as any other thing he could call collateral. Kansas did not follow suit when the majority of the country implemented the three-strikes-law. Instead, they put an asterisk in their law books for those who they referred to as perpetual offenders. While almost every other state sent anyone found guilty of a third felony to the penitentiary for life, Kansas simply doubled the offender's sentence, believing it'd be enough of a deterrent. As if anyone perpetrates a crime thinking they'll get caught.

Mister Drumgoole is an art collector, so to speak. Both elbows are covered in cobwebs. A spider crawls north up his neck from its perch on his collar bone, though only a single leg shows when he wears a t-shirt. A collared button-up conceals it completely. There's a coyote tattooed on his bicep howling at the moon encircling his bowling ball of a shoulder, which only works to make it look all the more rounded. His forearm boasts the black outline of a decapitated Woody Woodpecker, except it's not. It's a peckerwood tattoo—a prison tattoo—a symbol meant to let everyone know no matter what they alleged and convicted you of, it doesn't matter to him one bit as long as you are purely a white protestant or an honest and true worshipper of Odin.

It's hard to say whether he had any teardrops dripping down from either of his eyes with all the blackheads and as pockmarked as his cheeks looked. The last picture in his file showed both his left and right hands. Between his knuckles and the first joint on his fingers read *FREE HUGS*.

My going around with the title of surety agent or bail bonds recovery agent does not garner the same sort of respect being called a bounty hunter does. At least when it comes to laymen. Lawmen will snicker when they're called on the phone, or their door is knocked upon to let them know I'm in town and what I'm up to and whom has me playing hind-n-seek.

Some will not care for me because I am not a real cop. Others will not care for me because I am not protecting and serving but collecting a paycheck. Others still will not care for me because I am only poking my head around because they failed to do their job and feel as though I am stepping on their toes. What they do not understand is how there isn't much else I am made for.

When I was a cop in the Army, I did things thoroughly. When I searched someone's person, they did not come out of it feeling as if their rights had been violated as much as they had been sexually explored, lacking any secrets furthermore.

It was an intimate affair, for their safety and mine.

When evidence showed a handful of food inspectors were bringing in coke and pills along with the produce,

CID came to my door, waving a Kevlar helmet and flak vest saying, "Let's go, Juggernaut."

We hit five houses simultaneously.

At five-foot-eight and two hundred thirty-five pounds, I was something of a human battering ram. At twenty-six years old, I did not have much of an investigative mind, so I did not mind being used for my body. It was never me that gave way when meat met timber.

Construction isn't of the highest quality in government housing, to begin with. The lowest bidders never bring their a-game. They know they'll never meet the future occupants and said family is not too apt to complain about a free roof over their heads. Especially if they furnish the place with three times their annual government salary, and they've barely fulfilled the first twelve months of their enlistment contract. Simple math and common sense can go a long way when properly applied.

The kick plate on the front door sparked, and the doorknob came loose at such an angle the middle and bottom hinges stripped their screws. The inside of the door handle punched into the drywall and stayed put. Both husband and wife took off running but in two different directions. The husband went for the kitchen and presumably the back door where a military working dog waited. The wife went for the bedroom, as did I.

I wasn't about to stay in the doorway for any measure of time. It's what's called the fatal funnel, a place where criminals commonly concentrate fire when an unwanted guest attempts to enter their home.

In a stride or two, I had hold of the wife and brought her down to the tile. She balled herself up with her arms and legs beneath her. Nothing to cuff, in other words. I grabbed her by the belt loops and the back of her hoodie to snatch her up off the tile floor, knowing her legs and arms were sure to fling out to the sides, looking as if she was freefall skydiving.

When I sent her back down onto the floor, an explosion of black, sticky, tar-like, shit shot up her back and down to her knees the way a newborn fills that first diaper when they empty their entire lower intestines for the first time.

Both mom and dad did their best to bolt and leave their toddler with us along with a coffee table covered in I-do-not-know-how-many kilos of uncut coke. Several pounds of a green, leafy substance, stored bulk-sized coffee cans meant for the DFAC sat along the kitchen counter beside a food scale and enough baggies to keep the Ziploc corporation afloat for the foreseeable future.

All five found their way to the United States Disciplinary Barracks at Fort Leavenworth, Kansas— as did I. Though, I took the scenic route through Haiti to participate in the peacekeeping efforts following the US-lead intervention that undid the coup d'état that installed a military regime three years prior. The rules of engagement established for that embarrassing little episode did not involve supernatural elements, but I'll say without batting an eye that we did battle zombies on that island paradise. Doing so wasn't so much supernatural as it was extraordinary, much like when a cop comes up against someone hopped up on PCP, and they won't fall just because they've been shot once or twice or a dozen times. The zombies did the same sort of shoot-from-the-hip, spray-and-pray firing technique as the Iraqis did in Desert Storm, except they'd toss down their rifles as soon as they got within range of ours and amble off absently— no longer a threat—so we were no longer able to engage.

It reminded me of a video game, one that couldn't be won, one meant to keep you pinned into position until they were done toying with you.

One subtle difference surrounding my ending up at Leavenworth is how I happened to be on orders for brig duty rather than sentenced per a criminal statute buried somewhere within the ever-building pages of the Uniform Code of Military Justice and the Manual for Courts-Martial.

I stuck around the area after my enlistment contract ended for no other reason than my lease had not expired and because I was no longer technically a member of the United States Military, the military clause in my lease was no longer applicable.

Before rent was due the next month following my going from soldier to veteran, I took a job with a bail bondsman for the simple reason that I liked food in my stomach, and I'd grown rather comfortable around criminal types.

That's making a long story less so.

3

"WHAT CAN I DO YOU FOR?" asked an Underdog-looking deputy from the other side of the safety glass where he sat upon a stool and did all he could to ward off Mister Sandman.

There was a delay between his words leaving his lips and his words exiting the speaker that reminded me of a 70s kung fu flick. Adding to that was how the speaker sounded so tinny the voice seemed disembodied. I don't think I laughed aloud, though, I am sure my face gave him somewhat of a hint as to what percolated in my brain.

"I am looking for a bail jumper by the last name of Drumgoole. Drum-ghoul is spelled—"

"Yessum," he said and nodded his head, which made his chin turn into chins. "Junior, senior, or the third?"

"There's more than one?"

"Yessum. Wait a while for a good rain and another will pop up out of the ground, you can bet your ass. Like weeds. Which one are you wanting to pluck out of our soil, sir?" he said to me.

"I only have a birthday on him. Sorry. No suffix."

"You have paperwork?"

"I do."

"Hold on now," he said, smiling ear to ear at his own joke. "We just met. I don't even know your name yet. You should at least ask me to dinner first," he said and laughed. "And my mother will want to meet you, too. My mother, of course, being the sheriff. I'll buzz you back. I am sure one of our investigators'll help you sort things out."

"Thank you," I mouthed, despite knowing he'd never hear what I had to say and not wanting to waste my breath.

On the other side of the solid steel door stood a man in a blaze orange polo shirt who waved me into an office on the far side of the room. There wasn't an alligator sitting on his chest but a pistolero wearing a sombrero and a horseshoe mustache with a handkerchief tied around its neck.

I couldn't stop blinking under all that needling fluorescent light reflecting off those institutional white walls. The detective's neon orange State shirt wasn't helping matters any either. I can only imagine the impression I made with all of the blinking and darting my eyes here and there every few seconds.

We shook hands, and he said something. His name, most likely, which I could not catch over the bug zapper sounds of the lights just inches overhead. I think I offered my name in return. Either way, he let go of my hand, and I followed him into his office.

"Which bondsman did you say you work for again?" he said, unsure of why I'd been buzzed back to see him.

"Metro Bail Bonds LLC."

"Ah, you're from the City?" he said, closing his door.

"*The* City?" I said.

"OKC," he explained.

I shook my head and said, "Kansas City, Kansas. The one no one ever talks about."

"Kansas City? There's not enough of us to have spare time to serve divorce papers, as much as some of the guys here would like to make the extra cash. We surely cannot act on a bench warrant from another county. Another state's out of the question. You understand, yeah?"

"Yeah."

"You're free to poke around and see if he's come home, but we cannot assist if he gives you any trouble when you attempt to take him into custody. And, I'm sure you know, but," he said, clearing his throat. "If it gets ugly or out of hand enough for some neighbor to give our dispatchers a holler, we'll treat you like an ordinary civilian. No offense, it's how it is with your profession in our state."

"Yes, thank you, I—I am aware, and I know you got to cover your ass, too," I said, doing my best to come off like a seasoned veteran.

"Drumgoole's not one to stand and fight. He's a runner."

"Yessir. I am aware. Best I can tell, he made a beeline straight here," I said and set his case file down on the detective's desk.

"Would you mind if I take a minute to look over his papers and bond agreement?"

"Go right ahead. I prefer to dot all my Is and cross my Ts, rather than get shot by some deputy thinking I'm kidnapping a man."

"Smart," he said with a laugh and tipped his head to the side, lifted that same shoulder while scrunching up the corner of his mouth on that same side of his face to show he understood my meaning and where I was coming from.

I sat there while he pulled the file into his lap and read, skimmed, went over every scrap of paper I'd brought with me—front and back.

"Kansas City, Kansas?" he said with a surprise to his tone while he hoisted his left ankle up onto his right knee. "Here I thought he was roughnecking over in Cushing. Explains why he hasn't graced our jailhouse with his presence yet this year," he said, sounding almost disappointed.

"He didn't give his full name. No suffix, at least. I have his birthdate, though. Social security number and so on."

"It sounds like something Junior would do," he said and cleared his throat. "He likes to pretend he's the patriarch."

"Nineteenth of August, sixty-nine," I said as I read the date my employer had on file aloud to the detective.

"Junior is in the neighborhood of thirty-five-years of age. Senior's serving a life sentence for serial arson southeast of here. Big Mac is what we call it—in case you ask around for directions," he said, looking dead at me to make sure I was taking note of what he had to offer. "It's outside the city of McAlester if you want to see if he's gone to visit his daddy since he's come back—"

"If he's come back," I interjected.

"His boy, the Third," he said while he crushed out a cigarette he'd left to smolder in a nearby ashtray, "isn't old enough to be a guest of anything but our juvenile lockup—which he currently isn't. Unless he's been brought in during the time since you and I began our conversation."

"Do you mind if I talk to him?"

"If you can get him to talk, go for it. You're more than welcome to try," he said. "You've got his wife's information there. If there's money involved, she'd like some. She'll rattle off everything she can if she gets a piece of the pie."

"She's his common-law wife."

"Is that so? Interesting. She sure uses his name like they're wed. If he owes money, child support, or whatever. Work that angle with her. Sound good, Mr. Kincaid?" he said and stood back up from his chair. "If there's nothing else, I need to get back to my own set of problems."

4

THE ROOM I LET at the Golden Spur Motel wasn't what I'd call remarkable. The motel itself was a u-shape, three-sided affair, with a pool smack dab in the middle of what could have otherwise proved an ample-sized parking lot. I'm sure they liked to pretend the place was built in the shape of a horseshoe or a boot spur. I make that leap based upon the name of the place coupled with the one piece of art hanging in the motel's office: a gilded framed postcard of a thirteenth-century copper rowel spur on permanent display at the Metropolitan Museum of Art in New York City.

Fancy.

The first box I had to check called for a sit-down chit-chat with Mr. Eric Delvin Drumgoole Junior's blushing bride, Annabelle Lee Lately. The lettering stuck to her mailbox claimed her as a Drumgoole, though there was only so much room, so it read DRUMGOOL.

Her place setting on a dead-end dirt road meant I couldn't cruise by and count the cars out front or look for a Kansas license plate bolted onto a back bumper, or, spy, with my little eye, if there were any clothes out on the line belonging to an adult male weighing in at two-hundred-and-ten pounds.

If I drove through too fast and kicked up too much dust, everyone was liable to come to see who the idiot was that took a wrong turn. In that same breath, if I rolled down the road slow enough to not draw any attention to myself, I'd also make it obvious I knew I was where I did not belong.

The umpteen bird dogs baying at the breeze made sneaking up on foot out of the question. The one option left was to walk right up, knock on the front door, hope like hell I didn't get myself shot. Oklahoma is an open carry and castle law-abiding state, since the days the cowboys and Indians started playing tug of war with the Indian Territory. Had this somehow slipped my mind, the pickup I followed most of the way out to the house had a reminder stuck to the window behind the driver's headrest, which read: *INVEST IN PRECIOUS METALS* with an outline of a bullet and a brass casing beneath the words *BUY AMMUNITION LOCALLY at*...someplace in too small of a font for me to read.

I pulled a U-turn and parked on the shoulder behind the far side of a billboard with the front-end pointed back toward civilization. I popped the hood latch to display the international sign of car trouble. In the interest of thoroughness, I pulled a single plug wire off the distributor cap and tossed it into the trunk so no one hopped up on Hillbilly heroin could hotwire it in my absence.

I swapped out my undershirt for a vest that promised to stop anything other than a point-blank shot to the chest. Over that, I threw on a filling station shirt I found at the Saint Vincent de Paul secondhand store, a hand-me-down from a man named Albert.

Albert seemed like the least threatening name I'd ever come across. I'd never met a single Albert while I served, and I certainly cannot recall an Albert incarcerated in Leavenworth while I worked there. I am damn certain no one ever came in to ask the bondsman I worked for to post bail for a loved one by the name of Albert. I cannot say if I looked like an Albert, seeing as how I am yet to lay eyes on one, other than the black and white and tintype photographs of the physicist. But the empty one-gallon gas can I pulled from the trunk gave me a look I thought to be sympathetic—save the Beretta velcroed onto the small of my back, hopefully, hidden from the rest of the world.

After trudging along over a mile of dirt road with a handful of vehicles tearing ass passed me, tossing up an unwavering cloud of dust, I looked like anything but a law enforcement professional. I'd like to say that was the plan from the get, but that'd be an unfiltered lie. As was everything about to leave my lips meant for Miss Lately's ears.

"Is Eric here?"

"Who?"

"Eric. My car gave out a bit down the way, and I know Eric lives here, so I thought he could help," I said and gave the gas can a jiggle.

"The hell you know Eric lives here."

"Eric…Drumgoole. I've been by here before," I said with a shrug.

She latched the storm door, hid her hand and arm behind the door frame, and asked me, "Where do you know *Eric* from?"

"Hey," I said and nodded at her disappeared hand, "I

was hoping he might have some spare gas that might get me back into town."

"Does it look like that bastard has ever mowed this place?"

I did not dare look away, but I made of show of rolling my eyes toward the side yard before I said, "No. No, it does not."

"What do you want with J.R., Albert?"

"Is he home?"

"He might be. I don't know. This ain't home for him, Albert."

"I go by Al."

"You're full of shit too. That shirt's older than you." She said, shaking her head. "What's he done this time?"

"Jumped bail. Missed court. Left the state," I said.

"Who's dumb enough to post for him," she said. I responded by raising my eyebrows and letting her fill in the blank.

"I might be wasting my wind, but I'll still ask whether the two of you are on good terms."

"Nope."

"Why're you going around as his wife then?"

"Two reasons," she said, mashing her nose and forehead into the screen. "I want my son and me to have the same last name. Secondly, it's a whole lot easier to pawn his shit."

Right then is when I heard footsteps come up behind me. I closed my eyes and waited, and I guess I waited so long she thought I'd fallen asleep standing up because she cracked the silence wide open by asking, "Is there anything else you want to ask me, *Al*?"

I shook my head, told her, "No, but you might see me again." Then she hollered for her son to get inside. It was him, the Third, who'd come up behind me.

"Is my dad back?"

"Don't know," I said. Behind me, I heard the screen door latch flick open and Miss Lately let her son inside the trailer house. Then the deadbolt tumbled closed.

5

I STRIPPED DOWN and stood statue in the shower and waited while the water washed the red dirt the Sooner state was so proud of out of the crack of my ass as well as every other crevice it crept its way into.

The dust settled into my eyebrows so heavy I could have passed for a ginger if not for the black feathery mop that'd taken on the look of a drowned crow perched atop my head.

The only promises made by the Golden Spur Motel's roadside marquee was clean, cheap, quiet. I imagine they figured two out of three is enough to keep a guest from taking the time to pitch a complaint, though I could not say with any authority which category my pissing and moaning fell into.

When I first sat down to take a dump, I could not find a single square of toilet paper, but I shrugged it off and hopped into the shower. There is no sense in getting upset over something so silly. It is precisely why one takes care of bathroom business in a certain order anyhow. However, upon cutting the water off and searching the restroom for a bath towel, there wasn't as much as a washcloth to be found.

Butt-ass naked and dripping wet, I went over Mr. Drumgoole's papers once again while the weatherman went over an overlapping list of tornado watches and warnings to be on the lookout for as well as his guessti- mate as to how big the hail would be once it hit this part of the state.

Every square inch of Anadarko County proved a pain in my ass, including the neon orange pleather swivel bucket seat the back of my thighs, ballsack, and asscheeks adhered to while I watched the weatherman turn it over to the sportscaster and then some bug-eyed field reporter who brought the news hour to a close with some feel-good fluff piece I forgot before the commer- cial break came to an end and my eyelids grew too heavy to hold open any longer.

I sprung to my feet to offer old glory her deserved respect, confused as to where I was when the national anthem blared marking the end of the broadcast day. Though I could not quite cling onto my military bearing thanks to the nausea that floated up to my tonsils before it sank back to my aching balls that had left the comfort of the pleather chair at a much slower rate than the rest of me when I hopped up to render a crisp salute.

I killed the television set with a slap and curled atop the sheets in the fetal position, which is how housekeep- ing found me a little after seven the next morning.

6

I DARE SPECULATE that unfortunate cleaning lady laid her eyes on worse sights during her sixty-some-odd years upon this earth based upon her going about the business of emptying the trash cans, bookending the bathroom sink with the finest soap and moisturizer sample bottles, as well as making sure there were enough bath towels to last me through the weekend. She did so so quietly it wasn't her that woke me but the warmth of the morning sun on my shins cascading through the door she'd left ajar while she worked around me.

She left it up to me to decide whether to move and let her know I was awake, make the whole situation embarrassing and uncomfortable for the two of us or keep my eyes shut and wait for her to pull the door closed and take herself and her cart of cleaning supplies to the room next door.

I chose door number two.

In an unparalleled show of professionalism, which would later guarantee her a healthy gratuity upon my checkout, she draped another towel over some hard evidence of the X-rated dream I'd been immersed in when she first turned my doorknob.

A bakery and breakfast spot sat on the other side of a city park directly south of the motel. The trees along the way made for a nice shady place to take a dog for a stroll and a shit in the daytime but blinded passersby to those who did not have the $34.50 for a room at the inn or did not mind rolling the dice with the chiggers and the ticks and the mosquitoes or any of the forty-something snakes that called this place home come the evening time.

More of that insipid orange awaited inside the Shortstop Cafe. The Formica countertop, the upholstered seats of the swivel stools, the laminate booth seats, and the tables bolted to the wall between both of the booth seats; all boasted that swanky school tangerine or cantaloupe color everyone held so holy in their hearts. The place seemed a proverbial Grand Central Station. Young and old came and went. Traffic cops and transients sat rubbing elbows along the counter. Black, white, and every shade of brown in between, worked in or patronized the place. There was no better spot to been seen or disappear in Lawson, Oklahoma.

I seated myself in a far corner table meant for two people and pointed my back toward the dead-end hallway that led to the restrooms. Without my asking, a waitress brought a cup of coffee and a menu. The menu was typed up in courier font, meaning: someone used an old-timey typewriter, and that told me they had no intention of changing a thing. They did not serve dinner. Instead, they served supper—like the Lord's last meal.

The kitchen's offerings were simple and plenteous enough, though, the morning sun glared off the laminate covering, and the orange construction paper wasn't any easier on the eyes after I thrust my arm out as far as it could go.

"Need to borrow my readers?" The waitress said with a snort.

I blinked and blinked and said, "No, thank you. The orange is a bit much this early."

"Oh…I'll give you a minute."

"Thank you," I said and bobbed my head in appreciation.

She looked Indian, pretty as anything. Though I was thrown off by her green eyes.

Contacts, maybe.

When she headed back toward the register, I waited a fistful of seconds before I turned my eyes back to the menu. I watched her wiggle her way through the diner and saw no rear end on her. From that, I was sure she was Native to Indian country—like my mom. She, too, suffered from noassatall: a common yet sadly incurable affliction widespread among the multitude of the American Indian tribes of North America.

I kept it simple and ordered a burrito in case I had to take off quick-like.

"More coffee?" she asked after she'd filled my cup up halfway.

"Please."

"Waiting for someone else? There's plenty of room at the counter if you're alone."

"Oh, I am sorry. I didn't mean to take up a table. I was waiting for a friend of mine, J.R."

"J.R.?"

"Drumgoole, Eric. You know him?"

"If I was a friend of his, I wouldn't say so so loudly those cops could hear you," she said, and let me chew what I had in my mouth. Once I swallowed, she dared me to say something else while she scolded me with nothing more than a moment of silence and her eyebrows. "They'll watch you like you're watching everyone else in here, but them."

"Where'd you serve?"

"Hmm?"

"You served," she said, without question in her voice, "state or federal time." You're too comfortable around cops and got a leg out in the aisle like you're ready to run. My brothers eat the same way."

"Oh. Is it obvious?" I said. "Stillwater," I told her and wiped my mouth with a fresh napkin, "way up north in Minnesota."

"For why?"

"Cause I got caught," I said with a flat smile, which I let curl into a flirtatious one once I saw she wasn't spooked by speaking to someone she thought to be a former convict.

"J.R. isn't joining you for breakfast. I know that much." She said, leaning over my table so only I could hear.

"Oh? Did he call and cancel or something?" I said, not daring to blink or act too surprised.

"You're a lot of things. From here, you're not. Dumb, you're not. A friend of J.R.'s, you're not. Not that white boy. He might conduct business with you, but he'd never be seen with you around town."

I sipped my coffee while she said her piece. The cup covered a good bit of my face, which stopped me from giving anything away, and that was enormously helpful because, this woman, she was too easy to talk to.

"If you did time. If. You spent a good bit of cash covering up your jailhouse ink with some pretty art," she said, and let the last bit go real slow—almost in a stutter— after noticing how I watched her lips and tongue and the movement of her mouth while she talked, instead of darting my eyes from one end of the diner to the other as I had when she left me by my lonesome until she came back to my table with check in hand.

"If you're not J.R.'s friend, then who're you?"

"Simply a savage who can read and write," I said without meeting her gaze.

"I've heard that line before. Who said it?"

"Sir John A. Macdonald, Canadian prime minister—once upon a time."

"J.R. owe you some money?" she said as soft as she could manage while still being heard.

"Something along those lines," I said without offering anything else on the matter. I was being interrogated, and I knew it.

"How much?"

"Enough."

"Enough to hire some help? Must be quite a bit to get you to come all this way."

"All what way?"

"Please, '*Yain't from round here, boy,*'" she said in her best put on drawl.

"Okay, fine. You caught me, red-handed," I said and held my hands up as if I was under arrest, which made her let go a laugh, letting me know we were still on good terms. "Are you willing to tell me when he came in here last?"

"Oh, he's not one for fine dining. I'll tell you what—come back at three, and you can ask me whatever," she said and set the check down, upside down. When I moved my hand from my coffee cup to the check, she and I brushed fingertips. "Please pay up front when you're ready, sir," she said with a wink and an extra wiggle to her walk when she left me by my lonesome once more. And I did, after taking a final gulp of coffee and set the empty cup down atop a five-dollar bill.

I grew antsy waiting to get rung up. One of the cops felt it necessary to say, "Careful, Kaw-Liga. You might want to think twice before messing with her."

I ignored him, pretended I hadn't even heard what he said, paid an older gentleman dressed head to toe in that same orange. He walked so quiet and looked so camouflaged in the place, he seemed to have appeared in the time it took me to blink and do what I could to put the cop's imposition out of my head.

I saw the officer staring at me in my periphery, so I looked dead at him and corrected him, said, "My name's Kincaid."

"Kincaid, Kaw-Liga, Ke-mo Sah-bee, kind of all roll the same off the tongue," he said, chuckling all the while. "Mess with her, and you'll wish you'd done otherwise."

"Oh, I'll be all right. She's sweet."

"Sweet?" he said choking. "If you say so."

"She reminds me of my mom," I said, hoping to shut him up. I didn't hear what the cop had to say in return over the jingle of the sleigh bells dangling from the diner's front door along with the Jake braking big rig hopping to a crawl for the surprise red light at the far south end of the curve.

7

THE MORNING SHADE evaporated along with the dew in the time I'd sat inside the diner muscling my way through a breakfast I felt reasonably certain would hold me over until the same time tomorrow—unless, of course, the coffee jettisoned every other thing out of my guts out of sheer jealousy.

Traffic was light.

Most of the kids from the college went off to wherever they called home or found work for the summertime about a month or so before I followed Mr. Drumgoole to his own home of record.

Lawson was a ghost town.

That said, I had to ask myself if I were a peckerwood worried about getting my flight feathers plucked, where would I smuggle myself? The wife was a dead-end. Mom. That's if she's well-intentioned, full of inexplicable, unconditional love. The other side of that coin is how some mothers cannot conceive of the concept of being guilty of aiding and abetting when it comes to her own child who she has taken to protecting—something in the same vein of sacredness as spousal privilege.

"I haven't seen him," she said through on the plexi-glass storm door.

"He hasn't called or come to visit you since he got back?"

"Back?" she said, sounding flabbergasted at the thought of him having returned home. "'I told you 'no' already. Let me ask you something now.'"

"Ma'am?" I said, realizing we'd began something of a barn dance, and I was not leading.

"Did you tailgate him every inch of the way down here like them damn dimwits who chased down O.J.?"

"I did not," I said and shook my head wild enough to be seen through the dust engrained in the door and the film coating her coke bottles.

"Then how do you know he's made it here? You don't. You hunting, or fishing? Why're you bothering me?"

I didn't answer her question. I wasn't about to discuss or give her an itemized list of all the shit I had to shuffle through, deduction and detection I'd done over the preceding weeks, or the door knocking and bad acting I'd done.

"I want to see your warrant," she said, showcasing her impatience with my presence. I couldn't help but think I heard a suggestion of a hint in her voice how she was doing all she could think of to keep me busy while her beloved bouncing baby boy made it out the back door.

"I'm not a cop."

"What?" she said and leaned her head forward until the plexiglass door made a mushroom cap out of the tip of her nose.

"I am not here because there's a warrant for his arrest. He was arrested, got a girlfriend to pay a bondsman to post his bail, and then he ran."

She laughed in a way that led me to believe it was genuinely the first time she'd heard it, and said, "Well, Mister Not-A-Cop, who might you be?"

"I work for a number of the bail bondsman up in Kansas City," I said. "My name is Moses Kincaid, ma'am."

"You're not Officer Kincaid or Deputy Kincaid or Agent Kincaid or something else with a badge and a commission?"

"We call ourselves bail enforcement agents when we're testifying in court or working in or around the jailhouses, but that's it. I do not hold a license. It's not required for us or private investigators up in Kansas."

"What's all that mean?" she said, staring at my chest as if to let me know she could see the vest beneath my Royals' jersey.

"I'm freelance. A bounty hunter."

"Hell," she said and unlatched the door. "You sure quack like a duck."

"I was a soldier for most of my adult years. An MP."

"That shoe sure fits you, all right. Have you told his wife that bit about the girlfriend yet?"

"Not yet."

"She'd flush him out if she knew about the girlfriend. I ain't inviting you in, understand? but I'm going to come on out there onto the porch with you."

"He's not here then?"

"No, he most certainly isn't. He's not what you would call a momma's boy. Hasn't been since the first time his peter stood on its own. He loves every other woman he comes across, though—according to his own definition of love," she said, making sure the door closed behind her. I stayed quiet and left her words to hang in the air by themselves. It seemed proper and respectful, and she did not seem done yet.

"I haven't seen him," she said, waving her hand in front of her face as if swatting a fly I could not see or trying to rid the air of the unlikelihood of the idea of her son paying her a visit.

"He hasn't had much time for me since he got off the tit. I had to be a father for him, too. Eric hates his daddy. Hates to be named after him. I am sure he would love to change it, but it's not allowed. Not with his history. His juvenile record began before puberty ended," she said and smiled, pleased with her witticism, or getting off her feet.

"You can grab a seat, too, if you want. Not the wicker one, though. It's been out in the sun forever—far too brittle to stand your weight," she said and waited for me to move, which I did not.

"Not calling you fat."

"Thank you," I said. "I sat enough on the way here."

"Hmm…you still think you might have to tear off after him. Can't say I blame you," she said, and leaned back in her seat, crossed her ankles.

I raised my eyebrows in acknowledgment to let her know I was listening and going to let her talk uninterrupted. Still, she prodded. "Is it a professional thing, or more of a your people not having much of a reason to ever trust my people kind of thing?"

"Oh, that can't be helped," I said without letting on to which of the two it was.

"I don't suppose," she said and laughed, knowing what I was doing.

"Mrs. Drumgoole—"

"Oh, no, look it up," she said. "I divorced the sorry

firebug *long* ago. It's Forbus again."

"Miss Forbus—"

"Miss Jackie, please."

"I apologize. Miss Jackie—"

"Ask away, Moses."

"I go by Moe," I said, interrupting her this time.

"Moe? As in Curly, Larry, and…you?"

"Yes."

"Ask away, Moe," she said and did her best to hide her smile behind her balled-up fist, pretending to cover a tickle in her throat. "Boy, you got to be a confident SOB to go by that for a name. Or a stooge."

"Your son failed to appear at a sentencing hearing after it was deemed he wasn't a flight risk."

"Oh, there are lots of stooges in Kansas, huh?"

"You have to consider how we did not go and adopt the three strikes law like a lot of the country."

"And he committed another felony? That's why you're on the hunt. The picture is getting a touch clearer now."

"Yes, ma'am, by ditching court, he did."

"Not his third, though. I can guarantee you that for damn certain."

"It's not as bad as it may seem. Not all felonies are created equal. If I can bring him in in a timely manner. He may not be so bad off. It was a misdemeanor."

"What'd he do this time?"

"The official charge was leaving the scene of an accident, hit-and-run. A misdemeanor. If he doesn't show up at the courthouse soon, though, they do have enough to twist that into vehicular homicide with criminal intent. He put a pair of motorcycles into the concrete divider on the interstate."

"And they died because of my son crashing into

them?"

"Decapitated and twisted up inside their bike frames."

"Not a pleasant way to go."

"No, ma'am. It most certainly was not. The thing is, they were wearing full-face helmets."

"Mmmhmm. And?"

"They weren't riding sportbikes—"

"The fuck is that supposed to mean to me?"

"Usually," I said, "when one of these bikers—the ones with the three patches on their backs—are wearing full-face helmets, they're trying to protect their identity and in the middle of doing something fairly illegal."

"More illegal than running someone over with a car and taking off?" she said and scrunched up her face, folded her penciled-on eyebrows into twin mountain peaks.

"Unless they prove it was on purpose."

"If he goes back with you, the charge goes back down to a misdemeanor with a fine?"

"I can't promise that a hundred percent. I believe he's facing a month in jail and a fine at a minimum."

"Kansas got the needle or the chair or anything of that sort?" she asked.

To that, I leaned in, whispered, "You get your boy to come back to Kansas City with me, and the public defender might get a jury to come to the consensus that his shitty piece of driving might be seen as something of an unspoken favor to the public at large."

"See," she said and blew a cloud of smoke out of the side of her mouth. "Now, I trust you. Honesty goes a hell of a long way out here. The dust kicked up off the red dirt roads settles and covers the bullshit, does away with the stink. That's how come we live out here."

Without taking her eyes off me, she knocked the cooling ash off the tip of her cigarette and down over the side of the porch railing.

"I am not one to show my hand so early in the game."

"Who's asking you to? This ain't a damnable casino," she says through another cloud of cigarette smoke.

I laugh, and make my way down the front porch stairs, "The women around here are a special breed."

"Grab you one before you head out of town."

"Unfortunately, I plan to elope with your son."

At that, she laughed at me and choked on her cigarette while wishing me the best of luck, waving me off her property.

8

"A SUNBIRD, HUH? Turquoise, even. Still, it's a nice war pony," she said and pointed toward the back door and mouthed: "four doors?" while looking playfully unimpressed.

"Thanks," I said. Three o'clock crept up fast on me. Rather than standing the waitress from the diner up, I waited in the side parking lot smelling like I'd been doing two-a-days.

"Why not a Thunderbird?"

I smirked at that, and cleared my throat, "For the exact reason I am not wearing a Chiefs' jersey."

"Oh," she said and raised a clenched fist into the air. "Is there an AIM sticker on the back bumper?"

I shook my head no, opened the passenger door, and asked, "Where can I take you?"

"Nowhere," she said and waited with her best poker face for the disappointment to show on mine, which it did instantaneously. She jangled her car keys and said, "I smell like I have been in a diner for ten hours, and you smell like you've been working highway construction, so we're both going to shower and change and meet up somewhere later, okay?"

"All right," I said and closed the passenger side door. "That's fair."

"I know," she said and walked past me to her car on the far side of the lot. Before she slid into her seat, she added, "Get a Pistolero's jersey. People will ignore you like a stop sign."

"You too?"

"You've got my attention, cowboy."

That got me to scrunch my mouth, twist my neck, force a smile, and say, "I am not a cowboy."

"Indians make the best cowboys."

"Is that so?" I answered.

"What," she said. "You don't like poetry?"

I didn't know what to say, I squinted an eye and cocked the opposite eyebrow while her car coughed to life and pulled itself out onto Sangre Road.

I stood there for I don't know how long, wondering, *what poem?* when that same cop came out of the diner joking with his partner, who trailed behind him and sang, "Poor old Kaw-Liga never got a kiss. Is it any wonder that his face is red. Kaw-Liga—that poor old wooden head."

"Have you been here all day, officer?" I said.

"No, not…all day, but LEOs get free coffee during their shift, so…," he said as his stomach and chest jumped with another silent chuckle meant for me.

"You get what you pay for."

"Never in the history of history has anyone complained about anything coming their way for free."

"Perhaps you're right."

"Usually," he said showcasing the small-town swagger of a former high school piñata who graduated community college armed with an associate degree in justice studies. "Your date didn't leave without you, did she?"

"Seems so," I said, not wanting to continue the conversation. Instead of sticking around any longer, he said something into his mic, which got followed by a few seconds of squelch and the sound of gravel crunching beneath his Goodyears.

9

THE LIGHT ON THE PHONE pulsated brighter than the yellowed bulb screwed into the desk lamp. It wasn't the front desk, but the waitress's voice on the other end telling me I could find her at the casino's steakhouse.

I hadn't given her my name or told her where to find me. Nor I did not realize my slip up until I was back in my room, down to my birthday suit, and all the way lathered up.

The ability of a woman to seek and find is nothing if not biblically mystical.

I found her squeegeeing water droplets from the sides of a glass. The hostess seated her in a booth in the far corner of the frosted glass facade of the Cinnamon Steakhouse—purposely nestled on the other end of the gaming room floor.

"You weren't so hard to find," I said while taking my last few steps toward the table. Somewhat startled, she covered her lips, swallowed a mouthful of water, and said, "Neither were you."

She stood the best she could, so we could exchange a clumsy half-hug before I took a seat across the table from her. We shared a smile, and she said, "You look… different than I was expecting. I thought you were here to take my drink order when you first walked up."

"Thanks," I said and let go of a curious laugh. "I think. You look nice, too."

"You're welcome."

"Sass so early on."

"Again, you're welcome," she said. "Did you ever find your friend?"

"I went by his mom's place, but he never showed," I said, hoping to dismiss it as nothing that needed further discussion.

"That's weird," she said. "It's a good thing I didn't stand you up. Twice in one day is more than any one man could stand."

"He and I didn't exactly have a date."

"I know," she said, lowering her voice and bobbing her head without letting her eyes leave mine. "You know, I could help you."

"How do you figure?" I said, in an attempt to keep the conversation innocent.

"He might only like white boys, but he has a Pocahontas fetish."

"Is that so?" I said and let her finish uninterrupted.

"Oh yeah," she said, widening her smile and flickering the whites of her eyes in the dim light. "He certainly does!" She didn't change the pitch of her voice or raise her volume so anybody else's ears but mine could hear, though the exclamation point was there.

"Even with the green eyes?" I said, half asking whether they were contacts.

"I'm Osage. There are lots of us mixed up with landgrabbers."

"I was wondering about that."

"Oh?" she said without a hint of surprise in her voice.

"Mine are—"

"Baby shit brown," she said, answering for me.

"Oh, you have kids?" I said, laughing at my joke along with hers.

"Lots of little brothers and sisters, cousins. Lots of diapers."

"I am so glad to hear my eyes are a reminder of all that."

"Just tells me you're full of crap," she said.

"Oh, yeah?"

"Yup."

"Concerning?"

"C'mon now, you traffic in bullshit." The conversation was interrupted by an actual approaching member of the waitstaff anxious to take our order and end their shift.

Sometime before the check arrived, I learned the place was called Cimarron, not Cinnamon. She had fun with that, and I liked her smile and her laugh, so I didn't protest.

"My dad is Tonkawa," she said.

"Okay," I said.

"That's why we're at the steakhouse," she said with an inching smirk. "Besides, you look like a meat-eater."

"Okay," I said, again, knowing there was a punchline I missed.

"You're not from anywhere near here, huh?"

I swung my chin left to right and pointed a finger up in the air, "North," I said.

"Kansas City?"

"Farther."

"You a damn Eskimo?" she said.

"Green Bay."

"Hmm…never been."

"North of Chicago and Milwaukee," I said.

"I know where it's at, just didn't know they had Indians way up there."

"I'm Ho-Chunk."

"A what?"

"Winnebago."

"Like the RV?"

"Oh…more jokes?"

"We should go," she added, standing up. "Do you dance?"

"I cruise sometimes."

"No, I don't mean crow hop. I mean dance," she said and pointed toward the distant thumping sound coming from the other side of the mechanical calliope slot machine music.

10

SHE BOOTED ME out of bed well before the sun considered coming up. She'd showered and looked like a waitress once again. The air smelled of the vanilla-scented scrubs and shampoos she used in the shower. And coffee, too. The latter was especially welcomed.

My eyes blinked away the dream, and my feet found the floor. "Thank you," I said and reached to take hold of the steaming cup, which allowed the blanket to fall from my shoulder down to my waist and showcase the scars I had not been able to cover with ink.

"Holy…," she said with a gasp she immediately attempted to reel back. "How long did you serve?"

"What? Oh. It's okay," I said. "These are from a clumsy and misspent youth."

"Is that right?" she said and looked a little closer.

I clarified, "I never earned a purple heart."

Her reaction was one I'd seen from folks in basic training as well as a sprinkling of times like this one. She wasn't awake enough to pry any further, so she turned back toward the bathroom and told me, "I have to throw on some makeup."

"I have to find my clothes," I answered back, after swallowing a mouthful of coffee.

"Top of the chest at the foot of the bed," she said and disappeared into the glow of the bathroom doorway.

I did not bother with my tie or top button or tucking in my shirt into my dress pants. And with all the time I saved, I was left to wonder whether I should wait for her to finish with her makeup before I made my way to and out her front door.

I stalled some by emptying the coffee cup, then said, "Hey, Elise. You want me to wait for you?" though I wasn't so sure my voice carried over the sound of the exhaust fan. Had she heard the sound of my voice, I wasn't sure what I'd said could be heard, and I'd have to say it all over again, yell it again, actually, and it would come out sounding jerky and bumbling.

I felt stupid for asking and stepped toward her bedroom door as softly as I could.

Elise slapped the light switch off and laughed at the sight of me tiptoeing in her direction, "Why? Are you attached already, or what?"

I sighed, smiled, and said, "Just asking." In the interest of further awkwardness, I added a subtle shrug that came off more like a twitch or a shiver.

"C'mon then, Romeo, walk me out if you must," she said as she wrapped her arm around mine, laced our fingers together, kissed me on the neck right below the ear, which came as a surprise that made my ankle wobble some.

If this was a film, The Big O would sing *Dream Baby* as we drove off in opposite directions alone with our thoughts. I'd have a smile curling the corners of my mouth, and the last bit of moonlight would sparkle in my eyes through the windshield. That's my roundabout way of admitting she was right when she speculated I'd already become attached.

II

A KNOCK CAME to my door right around ten o'clock later that same morning, right after the breakfast rush at the diner would have thinned out to a trickle of customers— old men, mostly, slowly sipping coffee in no hurry to get out into the summer heat.

I saw an explosion of red when I opened the door to greet her. I heard a crunch, too, but I felt nothing until I came to in the bathtub of my motel room with some leather-clad biker sitting on the toilet, twirling a leather blackjack, pants down around his ankles.

"You're out of toilet paper," he said, sounding disgusted as he pointed the bulbous end of the blackjack at my face. Luckily, I could not breathe through my nose, but the taste of his shit hung low in the humid air and felt like fur on my tongue.

I could see the leather stretched around the outside of the blackjack was still wet with my blood. Blood takes anywhere from thirty minutes to two hours to dry. That was my window for how long I'd been in their company. I say *they* because the Basterds are a tight-knit group of motorcycle enthusiasts who rarely travel alone and who'd recently lost a brother to the reckless driving habits of Mr. Eric Delvin Drumgoole Junior.

Whether their patience wore out while waiting for me to wake was anybody's guess, but I wouldn't be left to wonder too long.

"So, you're not housekeeping?" I said, pointing a finger at him still perched on the toilet, hoping he'd take a swing at me with the blackjack, and I could grab the thing for myself.

Desperation makes you do dumb shit here and there.

"You're a funny fucker."

"He awake in there?" someone else asked over the noise of the television set.

"Yup. Hey, bring me something to wipe my ass with. See if he has some socks somewhere."

"There are some moist towelettes from a chicken joint," the other voice said.

"You are too kind."

"Well, holy moly, you're awake," the second one said when he stepped into the bathroom with us. "Howdy, Moses."

"Hiya," I said back and moved my hand to shelter my eyes from the overhead light in an attempt to identify the third member of our trio. The voice was unfamiliar, but my head wasn't feeling so good either. "I am afraid you have me at a disadvantage," I said, sounding as authentically apologetic as I could. "I do not recognize either of you. I have something of a headache. Sinuses, I think," I said and I tried to force breath in and out through my nostrils, only to see a crimson bubble grow and burst below my right eye. I was met with silence. Not even a sideways glance came my way.

"You're really shitting with him right there?" the one with the halo said.

"He was out cold. I figured, why not?"

"He ain't no more. He looks wide awake to me."

"Now, yeah. Do you mind taking him out of here while I take care of some personal matters?"

"What the hell have you been eating anyway?"

"Your mom's chili," he said.

The second one shook his head at his partner and told me to get out of the tub. Two and a half steps later, I felt like fainting, which wound up with me faceplanted into the carpet.

I came to while the first one kicked me in the ass and said, "Get up into the bed before you fall again and really hurt yourself but good."

I rose to my knees and said, "How considerate," hoping to make him think I was launching into another comedic routine rather than scanning the room for my pistol, but I am saddened to say I found it cradled in the lap of the second one who sat in the swivel chair between the AC unit and the bed, looking more relaxed than he had than when perched on the toilet bowl.

I put my hand upon the wall and groped the rest of the way to the bed like so, not wanting to crack my head a third time.

"Do we need to tell you who we are, Mr. Kincaid?" the second one asked me.

"It's only polite. You already got me in bed."

The first one did not speak up right away, he only twisted the blackjack around in his fist, wanting to give it another swing in my direction. "I never knew Indians were such comedians."

"That's all right," I said, propping myself up against the wall with a pillow at the small of my back. "I never found white people all that funny either."

"Fuck you!" the second one said and snatched my pistol up off his lap.

"You might not want to, I am—bleeding, after all," I said, knowing they had no intention of leaving me for the maid to find cold and stiff. They hadn't thought to hang the do-not-disturb sign on the outside of the door, a cue I used to convince myself it meant they wouldn't be staying too long.

"Does Oklahoma have the death penalty, do you know?" Harley Davidson asked the Marlboro Man.

"I'm not a hundred percent. But that is his gun, so it would be an easy leap for the cops to call it a plain old case of a drunken Indian committing suicide in a cheap roadside motel."

"Tragically poetic, barely worth a headline. Wouldn't you say?"

"Indeed"

"The thing is, the whole way here, I was hoping we could get creative with a murder-suicide. Unfortunately, he hasn't tracked down his guy yet."

"Yet," I said, interrupting their flirting with one another.

"Mr. Kincaid, in case you are unaware, my associate and I are—"

"The Brothers Grimm?" I said, anticipating getting pistol-whipped.

"You want to get the ever-living fuck beat out of you, don't you?"

"Sit down!" the other said, taking a hopping stride

toward his friend. "He wants his gun back. Do you think he is afraid of a few lumps coming along with it?"

I smiled at the prospect, but he failed to return my kindly gesture. Instead, he took hold of the lamp and twirled it in my direction, showing off his high school marching band skills.

When I came back around to consciousness, I was able to deduct how he managed to land the base of the lamp about an inch or so above my right eye. Some of the ceramic dust from the shattered base settled in between my eyeball and eyelid, mild irritation, in retrospect. I could not blink it away if I tried, which I was unable to. Blink with that eye, I mean. That's a roundabout way to say it took me some time to realize it was swollen shut.

When you wake in so much pain, the obvious isn't always so.

I could see my left wrist was lashed to the bedpost *way* up over my head on the left side of the headboard with a section of electrical cord—the one from the now busted lamp, I'm willing to bet. With the gentlest of tugs, I could feel my right wrist in a similar situation on the other side. Still, I rolled my head over to have a look anyway. I laughed to myself when I saw my reflection in the television screen. I looked like a slouching Christ on the cross. My arms were stuck in a Y.

"Hey, look," I said to no one in particular. "You're going to have to call the police."

"What? Shut it! Why would we do that? Maybe the ambulance before we leave. If we're feeling nice."

"If you go on over to the diner, you might find a cowboy. A cop might be over there, too. And I think I remember seeing a construction crew staying here at the motel. But this room is going to get crowded if you two have your heart set on singing YMCA with me. Oh, and one of you'll have to dress up like a sailor. Let me know if you want me to referee a few rounds of rock, paper, scissors."

"Are you retarded? Something get knocked loose in your noggin just now?"

"Well, then why'd you tie me up? Oh—"

"Look," I said, and rocked my head over toward the one sitting in the chair, who absently fondled my pistol as if no one was watching. "Seeing there are two of you, my safe word will have to be "Peanut Butter and Jelly, okay? Don't worry, I'll be easy to remember—you look a little soft around the middle, prospect, so you can be Jelly."

He flared his nostrils the way a perturbed gorilla might.

I looked to the other one and said, "Are you okay with being called "Peanut Butter?" you looked like you've had yours packed a few times."

Peanut Butter screamed at Jelly, "Goddammit, don't!" and I snapped my head back to my left to see Jelly headed my way with my pistol held by the barrel.

12

PLASTIC TUBING TETHERED me to the bed. I'd been lassoed with a loop that ran around my ears and right beneath my nose. Another ran from a bag hoisted above my head and had the opposite end stuck into my arm.

"What sort of kinky stuff you into, cowboy?" Elise said over the beeping monitor and the hiss of the oxygen. I blinked a few more times and let in the soft light of the darkened hospital room. I laughed, relieved at the change of venue, and appreciative of her joking at my demise. I tried to stop laughing when the stabbing started, but funny is funny, so my "ha-haing" turned to "ow-owing."

"Mr. Kincaid," a deputy said from beneath the muted television set in the corner of the room, "do you know who did this to you?"

"A couple of motorcycle riders."

"White? Male?"

"Yes, on both accounts," I answered and paused to clear the mucus from my throat. "You have them in custody already?"

"No, we do not. What else can you tell me about the suspects?" she said, with a pen at the ready.

"Assailants, ma'am," I said, correcting her. "I do have some compelling evidence of the crime. This wasn't self-inflicted."

"That's fair," she agreed. "What else can you tell me about the assailants?"

"Blue jeans, leather vests. Both were allergic to shirt sleeves. Basterds patches."

"Anything about their faces you could tell me, maybe, Mr. Kinc—?"

"Deputy," another voice said from the doorway, "he's going to remain foggy-headed and a little loopy for a while. If you could come back later, please."

"Okay," she said, clicked her pen closed, stepped out of the way so the doctor could come into the room.

"Mr. Kincaid, do you know where you are?" the doctor asked, leaning into what she suspected was my field of vision.

"Not the Golden Spur Motel."

"No," she said, "you're not in your room at the Golden Spur Motel. You are right."

"I'm in the hospital then. A hospital."

"Yes, you are. Do you have any questions for me? If not, you should try to get some more rest if you can."

I raised my hand as if back in grade school, pointed at my crotch, and asked, "Am I wearing a catheter?"

"Yes, sir." she said, "You have been out of it for a while. We can adjust it if need be."

"No. Please. Let it be. That it is there is great to hear. I was just wondering. I had a hot date the other night, and I was worried it may have been—too hot," I said with an extraordinarily toothy smile and rolled my face toward Elise in her chair over by the window.

"I'll let you be then. Can you reach the call button?"

I grabbed it and waved it in the air and she made her exit.

"Hi," I said to Elsie.

"Thought I gave you something, did ya?"

"There are lots of new aches and pains over here," I said.

"I'll let it slide, considering," she said, scrunching up her face in a forced smile before she let it melt into a look underpinned with worry and care. "Did you meet up with your friend finally?"

"No, some friends of his did pay me a visit, however."

"You party hard, huh?"

"Not really," I said, scrunching up my own face. "Some guys can't take a joke."

"You want to watch some TV?" she said and pointed to the remote control/call button still in my hand. I pushed the up arrow until the sitcoms went away and some olden music played.

"You're welcome, by the way," she added.

"Thanks," I mouthed with what I hoped would look like a question mark of an expression.

"I saw the ambulance go to the motel. I made sure your chart didn't say 'Doe' instead of your name. The deputy told me you're an agent, a cop, or something?"

"I am?" I said, trying to look surprised with my swollen face.

"Shut up, okay."

"Elise—"

"No. Save it," she said, cutting me off. "You can tell me later. They're keeping you till tomorrow. Then you're shacking up with me."

"I am?"

"Yeah, stupid. Good thing my dogs like you, Moe."

"All dogs like me," I said, and smiled, or tried to, and closed my eye.

"Maybe," she said and kissed me on the forehead. "I sure do."

13

AN ALARM CLOCK of Sally Jessy Raphael isn't the most pleasant way to be drawn into the waking world, but it did answer the question of why I was sitting in her studio audience while in the dream world. At least I wasn't on stage defending some inexplicable PG-13 kink.

While hunting for the button to release a drop or two of morphine and let go of my morning piss, I heard someone ask, "Did you ever read any detective comics as a kid?"

An unidentified, unfamiliar, disembodied voice wasn't welcomed, but in the interest of not being rude, I decided there was no harm in answering the question, so I said, "Like Dick Tracy and The Shadow? Yeah," I said.

"Like Batman. You know, the world's *greatest* detective. Because you look like Harvey Dent. Your face is purple on this side, mister. They sure did a number on you."

I turned my head toward the voice, but she was on her way around to my good side. I blinked to get the crust out of the corner of my eye, so I missed her until he was right up alongside me. Elise had gone off to wait tables at the diner.

"I am wondering if you knew who assaulted you," she said.

"A pair of Basterds."

"I have no doubt."

"No," I said and sniffed in a breath of the hospital's over-sanitized stink. "Basterds Motorcycle Club. Kansas City Charter. Eric Drumgoole—Junior—killed their Sergeant-at-Arms, and one other, then skipped town and out on his bond before he could be sentenced for vehicular manslaughter."

She put her pen down to her side.

A case such as this would be taken away from her sheriff soon enough. In the course of a single question and answer, it'd gone from an assault and a missing fire-arm at a rundown motel to involving a criminal organization from out of state escalated further by two deaths and the potential for more. That, as they say, is the plot thickening.

"Did you, by chance, know, or recognize, either of the two who assaulted you? It was two, correct? You said, 'a pair.'"

"Yes, it was two of them. And, no, I did not know either. One did know me, I think. He said my name, called me 'Holy Moly' when he first saw me."

"And when was that?"

"After I woke in the bathtub."

"Was he a bond jumper at some point, one who you collected. Or an inmate at Leavenworth, maybe? Somebody you served with?"

She'd read up on me, knew my resume line for line.

"I've still no idea. My bell got rang well before I got a good look at him." That was true. "I'd be happy to never come across those two ever again." That was a lie. "It's not like I'm wanting to go hunting after them." That could also be categorized as in inaccurate statement.

With the skin as swollen and tight on my face as it was, lying with a literal straight face came easy. And I'd like to think my monotone library/hospital voice helped sell my disinterest.

The deputy excused herself without further questioning, and a doctor came in right around lunch to discuss my discharge and the best methods for at-home care, what over-the-counter anti-inflammatories she recommended, et cetera. My stitches would dissolve on their own, so I would not need to come back for that. She told me where the nearest IHS clinic was if I felt I needed further, non-emergency medical care along with how her nurse would bring my clothes and discharge paperwork I needed to sign.

Elise stood quietly in the doorway while the doctor finished her spiel. With my good eye, I spied an oily brown paper bag in her hand, which piqued my curiosity. "What do you have there?"

"Leftover lunch special from the diner."

"Oh," I said. "Doctor, excuse me, someone else is trying to kill me."

"Aren't you the popular fellow," she said unamused.

"You're hungry, aren't you?" Elise said.

"Are you going to give it to your dogs if I don't eat it?"

"It's a meatloaf sandwich and chips. I feed my dogs better than this," she said and gave the bag a shake.

"Those aren't half bad," the doctor said, trying to hurry me along. "Sir, we need the robe back."

"I'm almost there," I said. "Can I keep the socks, though?"

"Please do."

I waited in the wheelchair outside of the automatic doors with the nurse while Elise opened the passenger door of her car. I'd polished off the meatloaf sandwich in the time it took us to travel to the pick-up/drop-off ramp. The chips were paper thin, flavorless, salted so bad you'd have to order something else to drink to bring some moisture back to your mouth. I pitched the bag and a majority of its contents into a trash can when I was wheeled past by the nurse.

The cops put my Sunbird in impound so it would not get stolen from the motel parking lot or otherwise pilfered while I laid up in the hospital. It wasn't impounded, per se, but kept for safekeeping as a professional courtesy more than anything. That didn't mean Elise was going to take me to go and get it just yet. I could not see much more than shapes in the distance out of my right eye. How far off in the distance? I couldn't say, so I couldn't see the point of asking her to help me retrieve my car.

"What kind of cop're you? A detective or investigator, right?" Elise asked, subtle as a tornado touching down while a freight train high-balled through a railroad crossing that cut the town in two.

"Not exactly, no," I said and swished around a mouthful of spit, trying to do what I could to do away with the cottonmouth feeling the pain pills gave me. "Have gun, will travel," I added, and I swiveled my head toward her. "More of a garbage man than anything else."

"Had gun," she said, correcting me, and spun the steering wheel to the right—hand over hand—revealing a field of broom-corn grown by the Ag students at the college.

"Had a vest, too," I said over the rumble of the engine and the bounce of the tires off the poorly graded gravel road. "And a badge."

"Garbage man?" she said after she straightened the car out.

"I get paid to collect trash off the streets. If they're worth anything."

She said nothing. Neither did I. Instead, we let the commercials on the stereo distract us from the shimmy of the car, which was enough to nauseate if paid too much attention.

"It sounds like you're a hobo collecting aluminum cans."

"Ouch," I said, and gave my head a nod of admission. "That's a—another way to put it."

"Do me a favor?"

"Sure," I answered back and sat up in my seat.

"Open up my glove compartment."

There sat my badge clipped onto its lanyard and leather backing. "Thank you," I said. "These are a bitch to replace."

"It was on the floor by your bed. In your motel room. I don't think they wanted it."

"Have I thanked you?" I said.

"Don't worry about it, Moe, I know you were raised right."

I let her think that and sat quietly for the rest of the ride to her place. The cab of the car was filled with enough racket already.

14

WHAT HAPPENED to your eye?" he said and tucked what was left of the pouch of tobacco into his left pants pocket.

"I caught a line drive at a Royals' game."

"Mmm, well—oof. I can't imagine how much that must've hurt. If you want my advice," he said and waited for me to turn and look at him, so he knew he had my full attention. "Use your hands next time. Haven't you ever heard anybody say, 'keep your eye on the ball?'" He laughed until he coughed and finally cleared his throat, then added, "I hope you got whoever was at-bat to sign the ball."

"Thank you. Wise words."

"Mmmhmm," he agreed, knowing he was older and wiser than me by any measure. "You're telling me you didn't get yourself fucked up by some bikers like my daughter said?"

"Is that a better story?"

"Getting smashed in the face because you couldn't catch a baseball makes you sound like a putz," he said with a shit-eating grin, knowing he'd knocked me down a notch.

I looked at the empty shirt sleeve dangling down from his right shoulder and asked, "Who was at bat when you caught that ball, Casey?"

He shook his head and said, "Charley," without a hint of amusement in his voice. He puffed on a cigarette loosely rolled from a page taken from the NIV Pocket Edition New Testament while he watched the dogs harass one another in the side yard. I said nothing, instead, I watched him watching everything and nothing.

Before too long, Elise joined us on the porch and asked what the two of us were talking about. "Vietnam," I said.

Elise looked disheartened.

"Dad?"

"Yes?" he said and shrugged his stump.

"Do you want to tell him why you can't go around the hay baler anymore, or should I?"

"That damn thing's possessed," he said matter-of-factly. "I had a whole story cooked up that I meant to tell him. I was acting like he had me stewing and everything. I would have had him kissing my ass, trying to apologize, waiting on me hand and foot. But you came out here and cut me off before I could really get going. I swear youth has no respect for our storytelling traditions."

"Good," she told him. "You two ought to get along all right as much as you both like to joke and bullshit people."

"Moe, you Tonkawa?" the old man asked.

"No, I am—"

"Then I won't like you. Give up now," he said, stopping me mid-sentence.

"What if he's Osage?" Elise asked him.

"Only one of them I liked was your ma."

"Whatever, old man. Do you want some tea? It looks

ready," she said, motioning to an old giant glass pickle jar warming in the afternoon sun.

"No, thanks," the old man said. "Your dogs pissed on it again."

"Are you sure the lid is on tight. It could have spilled over."

"No, it's sticky on the outside. Tacky."

"Sweet tea gets tacky, too, from all the sugar if it gets spilled."

"Tastes like dog piss, too."

"You tasted it?" she said and choked on the gulp of air.

"I stuck my finger in it and licked my finger."

"Inside the jar? she said. "Are you saying my tea tastes like piss?"

"No, I stuck my finger in the sticky mess on the outside of the jar and then stuck my finger in my mouth," he said. "It was definitely dog piss."

I laughed so hard I almost pissed.

15

I SPENT THAT AFTERNOON on the phone with Metro Bail
Bonds LLC, writing out every detail of Mr. Eric Delvin
Drumgoole Junior's file by hand on scratch paper: social
security number, date of birth, home address, home of
record, next of kin, marital status, all the aforesaid on
his spouse as well, vehicle information, bank information from the bond paid for his release prior to trial and
sentencing.

Guilt-ridden, he told the court he was prepared to
pay restitution and swore to plead no contest if only he
could have some time to get his personal affairs in order.

I didn't have a recent picture of his mug. The fax
came out so dark he looked to be of African American
descent. And my artistic abilities were nowhere near
where they needed to be for said task, so, following some
groveling, the Anadarko Sheriff's Office agreed to send
out a booking photo they had from a few years back. The
sheriff's consolation came in the form of how he could
rest assured nobody else wearing a badge in his county
had to dedicate time to out of state business, meaning:
the judge assigned to the case hadn't yet supersized

the charge of vehicular manslaughter to homicide and issued an order of extradition.

It's odd how if you stare at something long enough—even with one eye—you can still see double somehow. Or maybe it was the codeine the hospital loaded me up with as a going away gift on my way out the door that made my handwriting look like a 3D movie might when the glasses slid down to the tip of your nose.

"What size are your feet?" Elise's dad said to me and plopped himself down on the sofa beside me, causing me to slouch toward him some, stopping short of flopping my head on what was left of his right shoulder.

He laid his cane on the cushion between the two of us the way someone might with the little divider at the grocery store checkout when they don't want your stuff touching theirs.

"Mmmm…ten."

"That a guess?"

"I guess," I said, not so sure anymore.

"What're you hopped up on?" he said, lifting his lip the way Elvis so famously did, but with a glint of irritation in his eye.

"Doctor gave me co—dean."

"What, yain't been rolled before?" he drawled.

"Some bones in my face got cracked."

"Hollywood ain't going to give you a call anytime soon, but, lucky for you, Elise has a soft spot for strays."

"How's that?"

"Do you know the difference between a Playboy and that Jeffery Dahmer?"

"I do not," I said, indulging the old man.

"The magazine can take a beating in a bathroom!" he said and laughed without making a sound. "I wonder if the stuff would do anything about my arm."

"What? What's the matter with it?" I asked and looked over to his left side, ut he flopped his stump on the side closest to me and said, "I feel lighting strikes now and again. Feels like my hand explodes when the electricity leaves my fingertips. I need to numb it."

"Too bad, so sad," I said with a tongue that felt swollen and heavy. Heavier than it should under normal circumstances. I licked the air and did what I could to scrape the cotton off my tongue with my top teeth, tried to work some saliva up from the back of my throat to do away with my dry mouth, but it seemed someone turned an entire sleeve of saltines into dust and poured the whole works down my throat when I wasn't looking.

I coughed and could not stop. I coughed so hard I sat up straight without trying. I lowered my head, hoping the air was thinner and cooler between my knees.

"See what happens when you deny an elder something so simple," the old man said.

Elise walked in the living room with a glass of water and a gel mask she'd pulled from the freezer. I downed the water, one small sip at a time until my cough turned to a lingering tickle that slid farther down my throat until it disappeared.

She reclined me back, and worked the baby blue gel mask over my head, brought it to rest over my eyes. How do you spell relief?

The old man laughed and said, "Howgh, Quien-No-Sabe. Who was that masked man?" and I prayed he'd work himself into a coughing fit, too, but some prayers go callously unanswered.

It's all right. I'll just give him some Pan-Indian grandbabies. Joke's on him.

"Close your eyes and ignore him," Elise said, taking the glass back. "Put your feet up, Moe, there's nothing on the coffee table that you need to worry about knocking to the floor. Get some rest," she said and left me with the softest kiss on my forehead.

16

THE FIRST THING I got to see with any kind of clarity through my right eye in I-don't-know-how-many days turned out to be what I'll call an indigo sky decorated with neon pink clouds. Oklahoma did not strike me as all that bad at that particular moment.

I'd grabbed a pair of Yoko Ono-looking wraparound sunglasses of the gas station variety earlier that morning while Elise topped off her tank on the way to work. The purple discoloration left the right side of my face and traded places with a dark mustard yellow color like the fancy Grey Poupon stuff, but still proved unsightly.

I sat by my lonesome perched atop a stool at the counter that ran the width of the front window of the Waffle Hut and stared across the street at the Lawson impound lot waiting for it to open. Banker's hours extended to and were lovingly embraced by city workers as well.

Bottomless cups of coffee were made for such occasions. I don't suspect the Waffle Hut lost a lot of cash on the deal. Not with how their coffee runs right through you, cleans each inch of your intestines out better than drinking Drāno.

Before I made it back to my stool from the crapper, my stomach let go a muffled yowled in protest of its vacant state, forcing me to pull the menu from behind the napkin holder and hail a waitress so I could order the Whole Hog Waffle Taco. I made sure to make a show of holding my hand over the top of my coffee cup while I asked the waitress if she did not have any of the unleaded variety somewhere back behind the counter for fear of Señior Juan Valdez sending me back to the baño muy pronto.

She assured me she could brew some if I wouldn't mind waiting and asked if I didn't like the road tar she'd brought me before. I assured her I did, but it'd given me the shakes. I meant the shits, but I said the shakes out of politeness.

I suspect she understood me either way.

Either way, I'd grown accustomed to being half listened to, atop being outright ignored, by certain individuals who make up a rather hefty portion of the populace. Not women as a whole. I'd speculate myself and the fairer sex gets along well enough. The fairer complected, though, has not always been so congenial while in conversation with me.

Exhibit A:

"G'morning, Bruce Lee!" the man said, laughing to himself. I walked up behind him while he opened the gate at the impound lot, and I dragged my feet to grind some loose gravel beneath the soles of my shoes and announce my presence and not spook him. He was poking fun at my throwback sunglasses and the ambiguous ethnicity hidden behind them. I smiled to let him know I got his joke, made him think I was laughing with. Then, unaffected, I peeled the glasses off my ears and said, "Good morning to you, sir," giving him an overexaggerated head nod that bordered on a bow.

"Shit, Lord. Who'd you piss off?"

I turned my head to stare at him through my black, brown, and red bullseye of a right eyeball and told him, "I did not get a good look at their back bumper. But if you got a blue Sunbird in there with Kansas plates," while pointing inside the gate. "I'll start the hunt. I just need my pony."

"Oh," he said. I could see the lights flicker behind his eyeballs, "Out of the hospital already, are ya? Didn't expect you so soon."

"What," I said and folded my eyebrows in toward each other, "you've been borrowing it out for joyrides?" I grew as tall as I could to look over his shoulder and inside the lot at his back.

"No," he said and did all he could to roll his brain around inside his skull while he forced the corners of his mouth into a Joker's smile. "I didn't expect you so soon is all. The car's fine. Fine as it was when it came in."

"All right."

"It true, what they told me?" he said and waved me into the gate behind him. "You a bounty hunter?"

"That's the short version."

"Might I ask, why aren't you diving something different?" he said with a glance back over his shoulder. "Or put a cage in the back of this one you got now?" he added and swung his arm up in the air like he was about to go into a goose step but curled up his fingers into a fist instead—minus his pointer—signaling the way to my Sunbird.

"I've never chased a bond this far before."

"Well," he said, "welcome to Indian Country," and clapped his hands against the upper thighs of his jeans.

"Thanks," I answered back and paused for a smile and a look around. "It's nice to be back," I added. "When will you all be leaving out of here?" He couldn't see the smirk on my face on account of my popping the trunk, but I imagine he could hear it in my voice.

"No time soon," he said, and left me to look over my Sunbird. He left me with a song, an Oklahoma standard, "This land was your land, this land is now my land. Oh, this land was made for me, not you."

Prick.

My vest was gone. So was my holster. As was anything a cop might want an extra of on hand—or a biker might take as a souvenir. The only real concern was to bring Mr. Drumgoole back before the judge, make the cops and Basterds look like the inept assholes they were. Simple. But the ad-libbing, folk singing, land grabbing, impound lot prick made a solid point. There was no way anyone who did not want to stay in my Sunbird for a three-hundred-mile ride could be made to do so. Window tint would help to make it look less kidnap-y. I could do that myself. Unfortunately, I could not exactly get a police cage from the automotive section at Kmart. This logistical conundrum brought me back to the edge of town and the Red Dirt Chop Shop, owned and operated by your local, friendly neighborhood peckerwoods.

One promise I can make is how peckerwoods keep dogs as lawn ornaments and teach said mongrels to be equally dogmatic when it comes to the supremacy of their blond-haired, blue-eyed Jesus, which meant I would stay seated in my vehicle until someone got curious enough to find out who was idling in their parking lot, twiddling their thumbs, rather than bothering to come inside the office. Thankfully, none of my CDs disappeared from my center console, and *Hank Williams the Roy Orbison Way*, forever spun in my stereo, waiting for me to press play.

A knock thundered through the hood of my Pontiac and fluttered my eyes open. I stared at an ashen man hunched over, looking into my windshield, dressed in bib overalls, wearing a well-worn beaver felt top hat like Lincoln. But unlike the Great Emancipator, he looked more like the emancipated.

"You okay?" he hollered through the glass and wiped the sweat from his face with a canary yellow paisley handkerchief.

"Fuck me running," I said to myself and killed the engine. I sat there a second, squinting out through the glass, staring at this elderly gentleman who looked like he'd been carved from knotted mahogany, not sun-bleached pine. "The fuck?" I asked myself as I popped my driver's side door open and planted my foot on the blacktopped parking lot.

"Do you…work here, or were you walking by?"

"Own it with my son," he said and looked over his shoulder toward the office. "You alright there?" he looked back at me and asked again.

"Own it?" I said and regarded the painted outline of the cartoon woodpecker on the office building picture window, blinking behind my sunglasses enough to make anything moving look like it was strobing.

"Yeah, owned it for a while now. Awarded the property as part of a restitution agreement from the crackers who—well, you don't know anything about that. Kansas, I see," he said and pointed to my front bumper with one hand while he stuffed the handkerchief into his pocket with the other. "Let's talk inside. The heat's killing old fossils like me up in Chicago, so it sure as shit wouldn't think twice about doing it down here."

Inside, he invited me to have a seat on a cracked-leather

couch and pulled a pair of pop bottles out of the mini-fridge. "Sorry, it's sugar-free, but the doctor tells me I have prediabetes. I plan to keep my feet."

"Thank you," I said and lifted the bottle into the air, tilted my chin down some.

"You hear about that mess up in Chicago last week? Five or six-hundred folks died from the heat."

"No, I did not. I've been busy."

"Seven-hundred found so far," his son said, correcting him, from behind another desk squeezed along the wall on the other side of a row of filing cabinets that I didn't see when I first sat down. "Probably more with no family or people to check in on them who haven't been found yet."

"Seven-hundred," the old-timer said, tumbling the new number around in his head. "I can tell you right now there isn't another Sunbird back in any of my lots. I won't have much of anything for what you're driving," the old-timer said. Mounted to the wall above his head was an Oklahoma Sales Tax Permit issued to one Severenus Henry DuPree.

"Do I call you Sever—"

"Yep, that's a fun one for most to pronounce without having heard it said first. *Saw-vern-e-us*. 'Verne' for short. Or 'Pop' works, too."

"All right, Pop. Thanks again for the soda. It's nice and cold."

"Pop," he said, correcting me. "Here we say 'pop' and 'supper.' That's how we can tell a local from a Fauxklahoman"

"Fauxklahoman?"

"It's French-Creole for 'fake Oklahoman.'"

"You're Creole?"

"Grandfolks came up here from Louisiana. Now, what can I help you with today?"

"Have you seen the five-point harnesses they have on helicopters?"

"Sorry to say, we're out of fresh out of helicopter parts."

"Fortunately, they're the same kind used in race cars. Sport mods, pure stocks, modifieds. I think they are pretty much the standard on dirt track cars."

"Might be able to help you," he said, and I scooted forward toward the edge of the couch. "Might," he reiterated. "Got to understand, most of them we see are folded up pretty bad or burned out or stripped clean before we go get them. We crush them most of the time and get the cash for the metal. Most. But not all."

"I won't get my hopes too awfully high."

"Hate to shit in your grits."

"That may be what's missing from grits."

"I'll stick to my butter, salt, pepper, and cheese. Thank you," he said. "Okay, so what we do here is charge forty percent of the new original stock prices for whatever you pull off one of our vehicles. Fifty percent if you use our tools. Seventy-five percent if we pull it for you. Got to keep the lights on. We're not out to rob nobody."

"Got it. Cash work for you?" Pop didn't offer an answer. He just let my words fold into the air-conditioned recycled office air.

Two peregrine falcons perched themselves along the power line. They scanned the bits of grass and gravel between the rows of automobiles waiting for a mouse to foolishly scurry out into the daylight. Seeing them came as a comfort; fine feathered friends. I wasn't afraid of the mice, but mice meant snakes. The problem wasn't so much the snakes as having to separate the copper-heads, cottonmouths, timber, and pygmy rattlers, from the forty or so other kinds of slithering assholes who call Oklahoma home. Whether they could send me to the hospital or the hereafter served as the deciding factor as to whether I would go for the extra point—try to punt them over the fence—or if I'd have to do the high-step march that Saturday mornings cartoons made seem like the only logical action to take in their presence.

Dirt track race cars are boxy and bigger than most vehicles with bright paint jobs meant to ensure they're seen while winding their way around an oval track no matter their speed or distance from your seat in the stands. Billboards basically. Not what I'd consider difficult to spot in a field of sedans and minivans and pickup trucks, especially with hide-and-go-seek being my profession. Oddly enough, such a vehicle did prove difficult to spot, but the roof was twisted and collapsed from a rollover, giving it the profile of a Del Sol stripped of its wheels and tires, which I could best equate to hunting down a leprechaun amongst the clothing racks in a men's big and tall department store. The tell was how it looked like two pickup truck beds sitting butted up against one another: one painted a safety yellow color and the other an unearthly green, giving it the look of an off-brand lemon-lime soda can.

"I'll need to borrow a socket set and a pipe cutter," I said to no one in particular after I waltzed into the office once again.

"You found something out there, I take it?" the old-timer said back. "We were wanting to close up the office but thought we might have to send a search party for you. A pipe cutter, you say? Whatever for?"

"I can't open the door."

"You can't Bo Duke it?"

"The roof is collapsed a good way down."

"Okay, I see," he said. "I imagine the driver got out of that wreck one way or another. I doubt they left him in there."

"You've got a point," I admitted. "You're saying I have to crawl in whichever way he crawled out, but backward?"

"That's me saying I don't remember seeing a pipe cutter."

"You might be able to jack it up and get in from underneath. I don't know if it's a solid body or not. It might be a tub. It might just be a tube frame. No telling, really. That harness you're after is attached to the frame, not part of the seat, see? You can't yank the seat out and separate the belts from it and toss the seat. You got to pull the whole thing out," he said, dragging out the word "whole" to where I thought he'd break out into song.

Lifting it off the ground didn't bring me anything but bitter disappointment, but, fortunately, I was able to stick the jack in the door where the window would have been and widened the gap to where I could get through. It was a solid metal tub and felt like a great place for a snake to call home. If I was a snake, I'd like to live in a nice solid steel tub of an old race car—warmed by the sun all day long—where nothing could get in to mess with my babies without my knowing well in advance.

If people think those pit crews move lickety-split, it's because no one got to see me get to work on that race car. I'd say it's a safe bet I spent no more than mere seconds spinning the ratchet and pulling the harness free from the frame, believing myself within striking distance of a clutch of baby rattlers that didn't know any better than to give up all their venom in a single strike, let alone give a word of warning that you're close enough to burst their bubble, but it is rather hard to hear a hiss or a rattle with blood swishing through your ears as fast as your pitter-pattering heart can pump.

That's not to mention how the empty steel tub echoed and amplified the sound of the ratcheting wrench or every time I moved my foot or let go a grunt or shifted my body while working to free the bolts from the mounts. The thing felt like a convection oven, too, which got me sweating so bad it felt like I pissed myself.

How to get the harness installed into my Pontiac was another conundrum altogether. I gave up trying to fig-ure it out for myself and gave a guy at a machine shop a story about how my son was a vulnerable teenager and could not sit up straight in the car with a regular seat belt. I told the guy how I didn't want him slouch-ing in case the car ever crashed, so it couldn't be stuck in the center of the back seat because he could still slip out of the thing and right out through the windshield if we crashed at highway speeds. God forbid. I asked if it couldn't be mounted directly behind the passenger seat, caddy-corner from where I sat. I told him how my boy wore a helmet, so I had no concern about him hitting his head on the window.

The shop owner said three-fifths of it would most likely match up, or he would do all he could to make it, but the other two belts would require him to weld new mounts. I told him I didn't care how it looked, it was for my son's safety—that's what was paramount—and he said not to worry, he'd make it look so slick my boy would believe he was a real race car driver. After that, he

added about how he had a cousin with a similar affliction, but his aunt and uncle left him in the home for people to take care of, so he didn't have it in him to charge
me too much for the installation.

"Christ," Elise said, "lying is like breathing for you,
ain't it?"

"I deal with criminals who do not want to be caught,
and I did not think this gentleman looked like he picked
up his trade in community college."

"Everyone knows everyone in this town, Moe. Or at
least knows of them. If he doesn't know Eric from jail, he
knows him from school. They might be family one way
or the other. Married into or once or twice removed, you
never know," Elise reminded me.

"Exactly my point," I said and climbed into her car.

"Okay, Columbo," she said and turned the engine
over, "Is there someplace you want to go before we head
out to my place?"

"Ah," I said and searched my pockets for a piece of
paper I'd torn out of a phonebook. "Candy's Toy Box, I
think it's called."

"Excuse me?" she said. "Come again."

I fished a piece of paper out of my wallet and said,
"'Candy's Toy Box' on South Quay Boulevard."

"I know the place you're talking about, Moe, you per-
vert. You know my dad stays at my place all the time
now, right?"

"I need a set of handcuffs."

"I am not into that…, Jesus!" she said way too loud
for the windows being rolled up. I looked to see if she
looked upset. She did not. Her cheeks reddened, and she
did all she could to smooth away her curious smile from
the curled corners of her mouth.

"I need some other stuff, too, for work," I said, "Restraints."

"Oh, okay," she said in a tone full of amusement while widening her eyes and pointing her eyebrows skyward.

"Do you know of some other place that sells that kind of stuff?"

"I don't know what kind of stuff that place sells," she said with her cheeks blushing.

"Mmmhmm," I said and let go of a chuckle, as did she while she spun her steering wheel and pointed her car south.

"Want to hit up the Army surplus place first?" she said as more of a suggestion than a question. "It's kind of on the way over there."

"No, I do not," I said. "Those folks're leery enough of strangers as is."

"I am not going in with you at the toy store," she said.

"Fine then. Be that way. Sit out in the parking lot. Would you like to borrow my sunglasses, or are you good with hiding your face in your hands?"

"Shut up. I'll park next door at the liquor store."

"Oh, that's a much better place to loiter," I said.

"All right," she said, "Fine. Give me your glasses then. Are you so sure you want to go in there looking all beat up?"

"Something tells me I won't be the only one in there with bruises," I said with a wink. "It's a whatever-floats-your-boat kind of place, right? No judgment and all of that. But you go ahead and stay out in the parking lot. I am sure no one is going to recognize your car from the diner."

"Ass," she said, smiling through gritted teeth and laughed all the way through the yellow light.

17

"**ELISE TELLS ME** you two went shopping," the old man said and speared an olive out of a jar squeezed between his knees.

"Oh, yeah?" I said, "We got groceries and stuff. That's where we got the olives."

"And before that?" he asked and stabbed at a different olive.

I shook my head, hoping to change the station, "Errands, you know. Odds and ends."

"Odds and ends, huh? Whips and chains are what I heard," he said with a low growl that grew into a snicker.

"I needed handcuffs and a few other things and figured they'd have the high-end stuff, you know? Town's too small for a tactical supply store."

"If that's your story," he said, gnawing absently on an olive. Before I could say something back, he let go of a godawful, "Gawh!" and choked on what sounded like a mouthful of marbles.

The old man spit the olive into the palm of his hand, along with a bloody chunk of a molar. "Goddammit, they're pitted," he said and slammed his fist down onto his thigh right above his knee. "Mmm…sonofabitch," he moaned.

"What's going on?" Elise asked and hung up the kitchen telephone.

"Broke a tooth," her dad said, sounding like he was gargling.

"What? How? Let me see."

"On a damn olive pit is how," the old man scolded.

"Shit, Dad. You said you didn't like the ones stuffed with pimento."

"That doesn't mean I like pits. For Chrissake, Elise,"

"You got any aspirin in the medicine cabinet, or what's it called, Anbesol?" I said.

"Aspirin, I think. Yeah, yeah," Elise said while making her dad say 'ah.' "Moe, can you go and grab a couple for me?"

"How many?"

"A couple," she said and shrugged. "A couple is two, ain't it?"

I brought the bottle.

"Whiskey, please," the old man begged.

"Whiskey will thin your blood, and you'll bleed worse," Elise said.

"Aspirin will thin my blood, too, dingdong."

Elise gave him a trio of aspirin gel capsules, which he washed down with a mouthful of blood and spit while reclining the rocker back into something of a daybed.

A while later he woke, arched his back, and turned his head toward the left and then to the right, trying to find where Elise went. With her nowhere in eyesight, he snapped his fingers in my direction and whispered,

"Hey, what'd they give you for pain at the hospital when you got the facelift," pointing to his face in a clockwise circle as if my cracked cheekbone had somehow slipped my mind.

"Codeine," I said.

He snapped his fingers two or three times and opened his hand, palm facing up, looked at me without blinking.

"One," I said loud enough so only he could hear it before I got up and got the bottle out of my jacket pocket.

18

MOST PEOPLE WILL bitch about a backseat driver, but my Sunbird beckoned for one with the five-point racing harness installed all nice and pretty. Though I doubt anyone I buckled in there would offer any navigational advice worth taking into consideration.

I suspect, "Go to hell" might not serve as the most useful route to take between Mr. Eric Delvin Drumgoole Junior's hometown and the Wyandotte County Jail. I hoped he'd be the strong, silent type. Though, if he does get talkative, there's a bag from Candy's Toy Box with a few ways of quieting him for the duration. It might seem a bit extra-ordinary of a measure to take, but any highway patrolman will testify how a distracted driver is as deadly of a thing as a drunk behind the wheel. Unfortunately, this isn't the cowboy days when it was okie dokie to drape a wanted man's carcass over a horse's hindquarters and trot into town to trade him in for cash like a crushed aluminum can or an empty glass beer bottle.

I refuse to call such a thing a dead soldier.

I imagine the modern-day equivalent would be

tossing a dead man into your trunk and heading for the nearest FBI field office in hopes of collecting the reward advertised in the post office lobby. Any television show will clue you in on how well that works out for whoever is driving. Some lucky LEO will see your rear end sagging a bit, or you'll forget to use your blinker or come to a complete stop or creep over the posted speed limit, and they'll blind you with a swirl of red, white, and blue lights—and that will be that. Cue the music. Roll credits. Call the priest. Any last words?

I too will make mention of how this cat and mouse, peek-a-boo, hide-and-go-seek game grew tiresome. Especially, knowing I wasn't the only one who was *it*.

J.R. wasn't smart enough to give up hiding out in his backyard even with knowing it was in his best interest to leave along with me rather than the two Basterds hellbent on ensuring his breathing would become labored, to put it lightly.

J.R.'s knowing about the trio of us circling does not come from some crystal ball I keep in my back pocket. I simply refuse to believe anyone could be so dumb. Or deaf. It's well-known sound travels at a much faster rate in a small town than elsewhere, and abnormally so in a city clinging to the map in the middle of the flatlands of the southern plains, teetering along the rim of what was once the Dust Bowl.

19

ELISE KEPT TWO cattle dogs—Blue Heelers—named Salt and Pepper. Both bitches, or dames, I believe, is a better way to say they were both girls.

I didn't need to worry about which one was Salt and which one was Pepper, Elise said, seeing as how when you called one you got the other too. Plus, it didn't roll off the tongue quite right to call Pepper's name before Salt's. That, she said, was a bit of shortsightedness on her part. But the shoe fits them both, respectively. Salt was mostly white with bits of black peppered here and there. Pepper looked mostly black like a McFlurry blended with a few too many Oreos.

If ever someone wearing a badge heard you holler out for Salt and Pepper, they'd figured it was some poorly veiled code being broadcast to let everyone around know the police were paying a visit, being that they drove black and white vehicles. For figuring this out, the city cops considered themselves clever, smarter than the average bear. They'd call you on it, too, to let you know they were aware and unappreciative of your antics. Then when the girls made an appearance looking a whole lot like their namesakes, the officers tended to deflate their chest and place their dominant hand someplace else along their utility belt other than the hovered position above their holster. This is all coming second-hand, of course. I didn't get to see it for myself.

I was in the back bedroom waking from a late afternoon nap with Salt and Pepper and codeine when a cop let themselves into the backdoor and scrapped the feet of one of Elise's kitchen table chairs along the floor and plopped down hard enough for me to hear it.

I didn't hear them knock or announce themselves the way they're supposed to, so I was especially curious as to the purpose of this housecall, and, as I've been told since childhood: if you're going to eavesdrop; you damn well better pay attention. That's a piece of advice I'll never unlearn, which came from my grandmother, who was a professional gossiper.

Before the cop opened the door and came inside the house—uninvited—I heard another officer talking in drawled 10-codes to the emergency dispatcher in a voice slowed for the sake of clarity, combined with a hangover that follows working outside in the warmest part of the midsummer's day while bundled up in a bulletproof vest, drinking shit-flavored coffee and store-brand powdered creamer able to coat your tongue and retard your tastebuds so you can eat almost anything so long as it provides the calories to see you through the day.

I knew it to be a police radio the same way a priest knows when they hear the possessed recite Hellspeak rather than some poor mentally ill soul talking gibberish. It's a sound that will dry you out from a drowning death and tamp you down in the dirt of the here and now, let you know there's no time for a warm-up lap.

Déjà vu is nowhere near the right word for me waking from yet another medicated nap and hearing that voice of that same cop so full of questions, again. Saying it echoed of familiarity seems a much better way to word it. Time enough hadn't passed for the memory of her to properly embed itself into my subconscious. They teach you things like this at the police academy concerning the reliability of witness statements. It is why cops ask the same questions over and over again. Then, it came to me: the hospital is where I met her, where I heard that voice last. She was the one the doctor asked to end her line of questioning until a later date and time.

The deputy asked where Salt and Pepper were, which told me she'd been to the house before. Elise let her know the girls were in the bedroom, napping with me. "Those pain pills put him down hard," Elise assured her. It sounded to me like she was trying to shoo the sheriff's deputy away from me the same as the doctor had.

"Good," the deputy said. "The girls taking to him like so tells me I don't have to worry about him out here with the both of you."

"No, Dad likes him too. Won't let on that he does, though."

"That's something. Your dad don't like his self," she said with a snort. "Your bounty hunter boyfriend can take a beating. Wonder if he can hand one out as well."

"Don't know. Don't imagine he'd be chasing after criminals if he couldn't handle himself, though," Elise told the deputy. "Coffee'll take another minute."

"Oh, bless you. My ass is dragging, Lease."

She called her "Lease," instead of "Elise," so I assumed they knew one another outside of the typical police and private citizen's relationship. So Elise hadn't called the cops or had the cops called on her, so this was something of a social call, so I was able to relax a bit, so I needed to relieve myself as you do when you first wake. The problem was I wanted to let them believe I was still knocked out. I didn't want to interrupt their conversing. I wanted to hear what was being said back and forth out in the kitchen, so I didn't flush. Instead, I eased myself onto the mattress between Salt and Pepper and closed my eyes, so I could focus on the conversation coming from the next room rather than the sights in the room around me.

"Maybe we should become bounty hunters, Lease."

"What now? Like in, what was that show, Cagney and Lacey? Can anybody do it?"

"No, they were cops. I mean, like Simon and Simon."

"Weren't they private detectives, and dudes? Yeah, they were. I remember. We could be like Thelma and Louise then!"

"Shit no. You didn't see that movie all the way through, did you?"

"Thought I had."

"No, Crazy. Anybody can make a citizen's arrest, you know that, right? Being a bounty hunter is the same thing. Basically. Just got to work for a bail bondsman," the deputy said. "I could teach you how to fight and take someone down, cuff and search and all that like they teach at the academy."

"Please, girl," Elsie said. "I'll kick your dick in the dirt."

"Your ass'll probably end up in jail—the way you fight."

"What, bounty hunters can't bring someone in dead or alive?"

"Fuck no!" she said and clicked off her radio, "hell no."

"Coffee looks about done," Elise told the deputy.

"A big cup, please."

"You know where they are," Elise said and slid the pot back onto the burner. "I am not waitressing in my own house. You damn cops don't tip for shit."

"Sheesh, okay then. Grouchy, aye?"

"Hey, you turned off your radio. You're off duty. You only get free coffee and your ass kissed when I am at work. You're family here."

"Ain't that what they like to tell customers at the diner, too?"

"Please, it's only because the regulars *are* family."

"Fine—but for that, I am *not* getting rid of any more tickets for you."

"You bitch!" Elise said and laughed into her coffee cup.

"Join up. Then you won't get any anymore."

"I'll get right on that."

"No, you know what? I remember them talking about how they're going to bring in another dispatcher before fall. Why not try that out and see if you like it."

"What all would I have to do?"

"You know…"

"No, I don't. That's why I asked you, Sherlock."

"Answering phones and talking on the radio and stuff?"

"And stuff?"

"You can type, huh?"

"Not like crazy fast, but, yeah."

"Okay, then. You'd be fine. You could think of it like being a secretary, or waitressing: someone places an order, you write it all down, let the cooks know, and then you check in with them until the service is provided.

Then you do it all over again the next time your phone rings," the deputy explained.

"Sitting on my ass all day?"

"Yeah. In the AC without ever having to walk into a hot kitchen, Lease. Ain't it better than wearing a skirt and apron that smells like old French fries? Does your hair still smell like fried onions like my auntie used to say?"

"Maybe."

"That's gross, dude," the deputy said through a growl that came after she chugged too much and too hot of coffee at once.

"Whatever, which one of us is getting laid?"

"So what, cousin? You've got a drugged man in your bed. Better watch it. Might have to bring you in if we get any complaints," she said and added a bit of a singsong melody to her voice when she said "complaints."

"Shut up about my love life, aye," Elise said.

"Any good?"

"Shut up!"

"Give me something. Details. C'mon, I canceled my satellite like two months back already. I've got no more Skinemax at the house."

"No, you shut up."

"All right then, fine. Be like that."

"I will," Elise said with a giggle. "Ever think maybe he is only crashing here?"

"Whatever, you're not so stupid. Don't lie to me, little cousin. That's fresh meat," she said, and the kitchen went quiet. "C'mon…, you can't give me that look and then say nothing."

"Change the channel, Deputy."

"Whatever, I have to pee anyway."

"You know where it is. I am going to check on him.

He's been out a little longer than usual."

"Okay, yeah. Maybe we should have been whispering, Lease. He should be getting used to those pain pills by now, you'd think."

"I don't know. I'm not a pillhead."

With that, the doorknob twirled and let go of the doorframe. I acted the best I could to get her to think I was coming back to the land of the living right then as she stepped up to the side of the bed where Pepper lay.

"Afternoon," I said, and blinked, and blinked, while staring up toward the ceiling, and Elise.

"Good morning," Elise said back to me.

"Really?" I said and looked around for a clock. "Time is it?"

She laughed at me for falling for her joke and said, "It's almost time for dinner. I came to see what you are making for dinner."

"What am I cooking?"

"Yeah, you. I've been working all day, serving food. I'm all done with that. Unless you're paying me," Elise paused as if waiting for me to make an offer, then asked again, "So, whatcha making us for dinner?"

"My specialty, of course," I said and scooted myself back toward the headboard. "Umm…mac and cheese."

"Blah."

"I'm going to get going, Lease," came bouncing down the hall.

Elise put her chin over her shoulder and said, "Alright. See ya."

"Who's that?" I asked, wanting to see what she'd say.

"Cousin of mine came over to say 'hi' after work. Wanted to tell me about a job."

"Oh yeah?"

"Yup," Elise said. "Yesterday, you had me take you to the sex shop, and today I find you in my bed with two girls? Getting a little brave around here, aren't you?"

I laughed and petted Salt and Pepper.

"Get down, girls," Elise told them, but they didn't budge. They only shifted their glances in her direction to see if it was them she was talking to, not ready to end their afternoon nap just yet. "Hey, get down off the bed, I said." One hopped down onto the carpet and the other stood and stared at Elise and thought for a second about lying in the spot the other had vacated. "Down," she said again. "He's mine," she added and laid next to me.

"Oh, yeah, huh?" I said. "Don't I get some say?"

"Nope."

20

A LONE MOTORCYCLE woke me. I sat up in bed, swung my feet to the floor, and straight into my Doc Martens. I charged into the kitchen, tucked the bamboo knife block under my right elbow, pulled the cleaver with my left hand—then traded it for a carving knife—zigzagged around the kitchen island, the dinner table, the love-seat, the couch, the ottoman, and took a knee behind the recliner where I waited in its shadow.

Every now and again, something happens so artlessly it goes without notice. The fact that my boots were on my feet, and the right feet, was something that escaped me until I got startled awake by the sound of a polaroid picture issuing forth of a camera.

"Are you wearing a pair of my daughter's boots?" the old man asked in all seriousness while wafting the picture in the air. He darkened the window centered in the top half of the front door. It was daylight, but barely— the time of morning when old folks wake and begin their day when they need not.

"They're my boots," I said and stood, covered myself with the knife block.

"What do you call that color?" He asked, gesturing toward my boots "It's...pretty. Purple. Or what's that other one called, mauve?"

"Oxblood," I told him and slid the carving knife back into its self-sharpening slot inside the bamboo block. "They're oxblood."

"Cute," he said and sat in the recliner, put the footrest up in the air where he'd sit and sip his coffee while he watched the sun lift off the Cimarron basin. An old man staring out a window with his glasses still stuck in his shirt pocket said something I wasn't eloquent enough to examine at that particular moment, not with the evening I had. I could smell myself and knew I needed to wash off the sweat and the sex, and the carpet fuzz that was now stuck to my scrotum.

I goddamn near died when I stepped into the tub and failed to notice a bottle of Vagasil tipped and ran down the shower wall, leaving a porcelain-colored puddle of goo at the bottom of the tub right at the edge of the steaming spray of water where I planted my first foot.

The top of my head turned into a doorstop and I spent the balance of the morning waiting for my lungs to reflate while staring at a stark-naked lightbulb, which I estimated to be mounted four inches off-center by the time I peeled myself off the linoleum and bathed. Oddly enough, that was about the same time my vision became a blur, and I heard the old man complain about whatever on Earth had the bathroom door blocked.

"Out in a minute," I said to the old man.

"Oh," or "Okay," or "How about you get out now before I crap my pants," is what he said back, I think. I heard the "o" leave his lips and rumble its way through the door but become muffled by the sound of the shower. The rest was filled in by me imagining what would be on my lips if I were in his slip-on house shoes.

The water went lukewarm by the time I closed the shower curtain behind me—even with me turning the cold all the way to the right. The water heater gave up every drop it had to give, and I bathed with water pumped straight out of the spring-fed well that had a subtle spoiled-egg smell to it—as did I for the remainder of the afternoon.

I've had worse starts to a day, surely. Though, nothing comes to mind at the moment.

21

"DAYTIME IS THE WRONG TIME to go about ferreting out folks like the Drumgooles," the old man said and sat and cleared his throat to make sure he had my attention before he continued any further, "You've got to go after them nonchalantly."

"You mean 'nocturnally,' don't you?"

"That too," he added and placed a heavy green canvas zippered bag onto the end table. The stencil on the side read U.S. The weight and the oblong triangle shape of it told me it was a pistol. The box of .45 caliber ammunition he balanced on top of the bag insured me we weren't shooting the proverbial shit.

"That's a 1911," he said and pointed toward the canvas bag beneath the box of shells.

"Yours?"

He nodded, said, "It was my father's. Mine now."

"You giving it to me?" I asked without turning my head towards him, not sure of what was happening— wondering whether Christmas had come early.

"Yeah!" he snorted. "Over my dead body," he continued with a deadpan look to him. "You're a have-gun-will-travel type, aren't you?"

"I am."

"One without a gun. And you're not doing much traveling from what I can see, either. You need a gun, and you need to get on, don't you?"

"Yessir, that I do," I said.

"All right then."

I didn't say or assume a thing. Or reach for the gun. But neither did he.

"My goddamn tooth hurts something fierce," he said in a way that sounded like he was gargling. "Warm saltwater don't do jack diddly shit."

"If you want me to drive you to see the dentist, all you have to do is ask."

"Is that so?"

"Yessum."

"He'll charge me fifty bucks to open up and say ahh."

"So," I said and pointed toward where the pistol lay, "do you want me to take you out back and put you out of your misery?"

"That doesn't sound so bad," he said. "Do you have any more of whatever they gave you for your face?"

"I believe so. Why? Would you like another?"

"If you would, please. If you're not running low."

"No, it's all right," I said.

I returned from Elise's bedroom with the pill bottle in hand and shook a single tablet into his outstretched palm. "Oh, bless you," he said and brought his hand to his face so fast you'd swear he was about to render a crisp salute.

"Water?"

"No need. Already down the hatch," he said and stuck his tongue out, showing the chalky white streak trailing toward his tonsils. I lifted my eyebrows as high as they could go to let him know I'd saw plenty, hoping he'd get the hint to reel the thing back into his head.

He pulled back on a lever that sent his feet flying up into the air almost before I could step out of the way. He let go of a laugh while I twisted the cap back onto the bottle, uncrossed my feet, and began my way back towards the bedroom. "Oh, no. Leave the bottle, Barkeep," he said, placing his one hand atop mine.

"Where you going now?" the old man asked me.

"I need a glass of water," I said and gulped down a mouthful of nothing while walking into the kitchen. "I've got a flavor in the back of my throat."

"I see."

"You do, huh? I haven't eaten all day," I told him.

"Water ain't going to fix it. Make you some lunch."

"You hungry?" I asked and peeled open a cabinet door.

"Nope. Thanks. I'm sleepy as all hell, though."

"I can't imagine why," I said to myself and closed the cabinet door before I peered inside the refrigerator.

"Slap something between two slices of bread and get back in here so I can show you this Government Colt. It ain't dummy-proof like what the Army uses these days."

"Is that so?" I said, still staring into the fridge, pausing between each word, wondering whether he was calling me a dummy or merely repeating something he'd heard his father say one time too many.

"Yep. Grab something out of the crisper, too. You'll live longer."

"All right."

"Surprised you haven't died of scurvy, eating the way you do."

"You're not wrong," I said, not specifying what I was referring to, nor being sure myself.

"Thanks. Now tell me something I do not know."

I contemplated telling something concerning his daughter's bedroom proclivities, but he had the gun in hand. I kept chewing and offered him a tickled smile instead.

"Finish your sandwich and wash your hands before you touch this, understand?"

"Yup," I muttered with a mouthful of wonder bread clinging to the roof of my mouth.

He dropped the magazine and released all the safeties before he went over all the interlocking plugs and pins until he had it laying in two pieces: the upper and lower.

"I trust you know how to clean a pistol."

"I do, indeed."

"All right. I'm going sit right here and watch you put it back the way it was, and you're not taking it anywhere until you do it the proper way, got it?"

"Got it."

"All right," he said and lobbed another codeine tablet onto his tongue. "Let's see if you were paying attention."

By the time I pointed the pistol toward the coffee table to perform a functions check, his lights were all still on, but nobody was home. He wasn't sleeping from what I could tell unless he did so with his eyes opened. He wasn't blinking or reacting to anything I said or did—not even when I loaded the magazine to capacity, seated it, sent the slide home, and said, "Merry Christmas, to me," admiring a piece of weaponry that had gone unchanged as long as the great white shark.

22

GAS WAS A BUCK-FIFTEEN a gallon, so I had to break a ten-dollar-bill to top off my tank. It should have cost me one hell of a lot less with all the pump jacks people had as lawn ornaments.

Gas stations are another place where one can loiter with out-of-state plates without anyone taking note, no matter if it's right off the highway or in the middle of historic downtown Lawson. Especially if what you're driving is nothing special. Even more so if you happen to be dark-haired and dark complected.

You can buy a bag of chips, a chicken salad sandwich, and one of those fountain drinks that are too damn big to fit inside any cup holder ever made and sit and watch the passing cars for hours on end with no one becoming the wiser. Most everyone else gets their gas, drains their bladder, fills up on snacks, buys a lotto ticket or two, and gets out of there as fast as they can manage.

The only ones who'll notice you are the ones who came there on foot and have no intention of talking to anyone with a badge, no matter the sort. They'll ignore you right along with the warning sign that reads: no soliciting. You have to look like the sort of person no drunk or dusthead would ever want to ask for any spare coinage from, so you can't simply toss a pistol onto the dashboard because someone else will get it in their head how you're there to hold up the place and they'll call the cops. Instead, you have to fix your face in a way that reads: fuck off and looks incapable of expressing any other human emotion. The Army calls this *military bearing*, and, luckily, I am still steeped in the practice.

Prisons use bloodhounds and helicopters and duly commissioned marshals for this sort of work. But here I sit, playing peek-a-boo, hide-and-go-seek, and all I keep wondering is what Olly-Olly-oxen-free meant when it was first coined. I mean, was it co-opted from something else, or was it something a bunch mush-mouthed kids came up with while conversing with a puppet sitting on a sixty-year-old man's hand on a black and white television show back when colored was an okay thing to call folks possessing a particular pigmentation but not to be born as such? Those would be the same sort of kids who'd wear fake feathers on their heads and played Indian. Meanwhile, my grandparents got a bowl plopped atop their heads and had everything sticking out chopped off so as to take on as much of the appearance of Timmy and Bobby and little Johnny as possible.

I need to find a book on tape for days like this one.

I bet I could pick up a tip or two from Sherlock Holmes. Surely there's something in his collected works I haven't thought of for myself. He had Watson. Someone to talk to might help. Or maybe a hound like in the Baskervilles book. The thing probably eats like it has a tapeworm and craps like a truck driver. Farts like one, too, I bet.

No thank you.

Two city cops on black and white Harleys passed by a little after two-thirty, then again at the top of the hour. Both of them shifted and throttled in a way that was no good for a bike, not that they put a penny into the purchase or upkeep. It was more of a look-at-me, look-at-me, display of horsepower meant to impress a group of college-aged ladies waiting on the sidewalk for the light to change. Their chin straps were on so tight they couldn't have returned a smile from any one of those women if they wanted. Instead, they looked like they were holding in a log their v-twins and morning coffee wanted to jiggle out of them. They were circling the way sharks do, waiting for their shift to come to an end—not protecting or serving, but not doing the best job of lying in wait, either.

Take away the guns and the badges and about ten years, and it would be pretty easy to imagine them patrolling the high school cafeteria for some kid half their size to punch and kick and trip the same way their dads did to them when they didn't make the football team again.

With those two knuckleheads on the prowl, I knew the probability of me seeing who I was looking for was somewhere between slim to none. That's not to mention, I'd done away with 48oz of Jolt and had to piss so bad I could taste it, making my attention span equivalent to that of a metal flake paint huffer.

Staying put in the car and refilling the styrofoam cup wasn't an option seeing as how the Jolt was sitting on top of more cups of coffee than I could count, and I did not wish for my cup to overfloweth. Nor did I want to show my face inside the gas station once again and strike the clerk with déjà vu, so I pointed my car east into a less populated part of town and found another filling station where I parked beneath the canopy to keep my car as cool as I could.

"Bathroom's for paying customers only."

"I'll be topping off my tank, I just need to drain my bladder first," I said to the fucknuckle behind the counter.

"If you say so…sir…you'll need the key," he said.

"All right, where is it hiding?"

"You'll have to prepay for that gas."

"I could always piss in the trash cash while I am pumping gas."

"Wouldn't be the first time," he said unamused.

"Fuck. How much are hot dogs?"

"Free with a full tank of gas."

"Shit, I can't win, can I? Here's a dollar. Can I go piss now?"

He shook his head, said, "Need seven more cents from you."

"Goddamn, you. Here's a five. That enough?"

"That'll do," he said and slid the cartoonish keyring across the counter in slow motion.

I power walked my way toward the restroom sign and ignored him when he asked if I'd like chili on my hot dogs. Plural. They were a half dozen for five bucks. The chili sauce was complimentary.

I pissed so long they went cold by the time I returned the bathroom key to him. "You got something against folks like me? Indians?" I said, instead of what I wanted to—what I practiced while pissing.

"Indian? I hadn't a clue, sir. You could be from anywhere."

"Well, I am from here."

"Oh, you're not in Kansas anymore, Toto." He said, looking out at my Pontiac parked beside his only pump. "How much do you want to put on the pump?"

"I just wanted to take a piss."

He smirked and slid a sack full of chill dogs toward me. Then when I stepped out the door, I heard him say, "Have a nice day, Tonto," over the ding that sounded each time a customer crossed the threshold.

"Excuse me?" I said, turning on my heel. "I didn't catch the last bit you said there."

"Have a nice day, Toto. You know, Kansas, Toto, *Wizard of Oz*, and all of that."

"If you only had a brain," I added under my breath and let the door shut on its own.

23

THE HALFWAY HOUSE sits smackdab between Oklahoma City and Tulsa. It's a forty-five-minute drive to the city limits of either place or a forty-five-minute straight shot from the southeastern edge of Lawson—if anyone cared enough to try to triangulate where I'd wound up, that is.

How I'd wound up there is I'd followed a vehicle that looked a lot like the one J.R. drove the night he turned two motorcycles into one big pile of twisted metal and charred leather that stunk of undercooked meat and warm road tar. There were two bodies mixed into the pile, too, though they weren't identifiable as such. The Firefighters killed their lights while cleaning up the mess, so rubberneckers wouldn't notice the mother of pearl-colored swirls atop the leaked pools of gasoline and engine oil had a deep red, almost maroon, hue to it.

All the aforesaid should have been called to mind when I peeled open the bun and splattered ketchup atop the medium-rare-grilled ground meat and the sweating, caramelized onions. Maybe it was, and it just wasn't enough to turn my stomach the way it would with more sensitive folks. Or maybe I was hungry and had not a care concerning off-putting images of roadkill. Or maybe I sided somewhat more with J.R. than two dead bikers after their brothers did what they could to turn my face from convex to concave. Or maybe I'd become distracted by a poster advertising the upcoming Oklahoma State Prison Rodeo held annually in McAlester, Oklahoma, home of the state penitentiary affectionately known as Big Mac, also home of Mr. Eric Delvin Drumgoole Senior—arsonist extraordinaire.

I put two and two together and scooted back from my plate so fast the bartender asked me if everything wasn't all right.

"Oh, bit my cheek is all. But, while I got your attention," I said and waved a finger at the poster, "I was wondering if that's worth the drive."

"Prison rodeo? It's worth watching. I haven't been in a handful of years."

"Anybody ever make a run for it in the middle of it all?"

"Try to escape, you mean? They've pulled some stunts down there, but I don't think they've ever done anything to jeopardize a day of fresh air. They're locked down permanently at that place."

I took a swig off my drink, cleared my throat, and asked what he meant by *permanently*.

"There was a real bad riot a few years back, maybe ten years ago now. They burned most of the place to the ground while I was in high school. Gutted a good bit of it, at least. Hell, once upon a time, they killed a warden."

"Hmm, if one of them gets stomped by a bull, the guards, they don't let go any tears."

"Oh, no, don't get me wrong, it's a legit rodeo—for the most part. Every event you can conjure. They bring in prisoners from other places around the state. The women's prison sends inmates, too."

"Fun."

"You want another?" he said and pulled the pint glass I'd emptied off the bar.

"Nah. I need to get going soon as I kill off these fries," I told him. "Water, please."

"I'll grab your check, too," he said.

I replied with a single slow nod while swallowing the last bite of the burger on my plate.

24

WHEN I PULLED INTO Elise's place, it was already black out-side, but it might as well have been the middle of the day. The old man's recliner sat in her driveway, kindling flames tall enough to see as soon as I turned the corner.

Elise sat on the ground, hugging Salt and Pepper with one arm each leaned back against her cousin, the dep-uty's, shins. The deputy squeezed Elise's neck with one hand and leaned against the front fender of her patrol car she pulled off onto the shoulder of the road running alongside Elise's place.

Elise's eyes were wet, glistening from the thick smoke coming off the burning styrofoam cushioning, which once made the recliner the most comfortable place to sit in the whole house.

"What did the chair do?" I said instead of hello.

"My dad shit all over it," Elise answered.

"What now?" I said, but Elise erupted into even greater tears.

"It looked like he took a good bit of your pain pills," the cousin said, answering for Elise. "The codeine."

I didn't want to ask, but I did, "Where is he now?"

"Funeral home," Elise said.

"The hell?"

"Lungs and heart gave out, most likely. Some folks slip into a coma, others pass when they take too much," the cousin said. "It happens more and more all the time. Docs keep handing out those pills to anyone. Like they're aspirin. When someone takes too many like that, it'll make the pulse shallow, hard to find. But they couldn't even shock him back. He was gone for a while before she found him."

"He had a—cracked tooth that was hurting him pretty badly, so I let him have one before I took off," I told the cousin. Elise turned her head to look my way for the first time since I walked up on the two of them.

"How many?" Elise asked.

"One."

"There's about six left in the bottle," Elise said, sounding like she was correcting me.

"No, that doesn't sound right. I—I had a lot more than that left. The doctor gave me almost a full month's worth. It ain't been but what, two, two and a half weeks at most?"

"What time did you leave him?"

"I can't remember off the top of my head."

"Where were you anyway?"

"I went to look for J.R., Drumgoole, I mean. I thought I found his truck."

"Did you?"

"Wasn't him driving, maybe the wife. We hit the toll-way, and I was about three cars back when we hit the toll booth."

"Wife…," Elise said and sniffed back her tears and dripping nose.

"Come on, girlie, let's find you some alcohol."

"That sounds magnificent," Elise said.

"Hey, Boba Fett," the cousin said. "Will you watch the fire while I bring her inside?"

"Yeah, I got this," I said. "Boba Fett, huh?" I said. "Clever." I smiled, so did the cousin. Though she added a shrug to hers.

"I don't care much for cowboys. I know Indians. I don't know any other famous bounty hunters. They're sort of like freelance lawmen. They don't exactly get their own schoolhouse lessons or tv shows. They're more of what's added to give a western some grit and consequence after the bad guy makes his escape. He's goodness for the sake of greed," the cousin said over her shoulder while she walked Elise up onto the porch.

"Given this some thought, I'd say."

"Have you given this any thought?" the cousin said, motioning toward Elise while she walked through the front door. I stayed quiet. The cousin waited for the door to close before she continued what she had to say to me, "Or are you just playing house?"

She didn't wait for me to answer, instead, she twisted the doorknob and joined Elise inside for the festivities and mourning.

25

I PICKED WHAT didn't burn out of the pile of ash: metal springs and straps, mostly. What did burn, I shoveled as much of it as I could into the trash can once it cooled. The rest I swept into the ditch. Then I went about rearranging the furniture so Elise wouldn't be greeted by the big cavity where the old man's recliner once stood. The diner knew better than to expect her to come into work that morning. The two cousins slept together in the bed, and I did what I could to get comfortable on the loveseat.

The deputy got summoned out of the back bedroom by the smell of coffee filling the and caught me surveying the newly situated living room.

"You're a good man, Charlie Brown."

"G'morning," I said, not yet realizing who was talking to me.

I blinked a bunch and looked over toward the coffee pot where the deputy stood pouring herself a mug. "No, really, you're alright. A little weird, but the military does that to people."

"Excuse me?"

"You didn't have to stick around with all that mess

going on last night. But you did, and you even went
and moved the living room around so she wouldn't be
slapped in the face with the giant hole where my uncle
would have his ass planted any other day. You didn't have
to do that, and you didn't wait for anyone to ask you to
do it." She didn't say anything more. Instead, she sipped
her coffee and kept her eyes fixed on me.

That weekend, there was a wake for the old man,
closed casket. Not for the normal reasons, however, but
because he wasn't embalmed. He wanted to become part
of the land, not further poison it with all the chemicals
they pump the dead people full of—his words. It shaped
up to be a typical affair: out-of-context scripture, followed by finger sandwiches and funny stories. Very little
crying. Indians have an incurable habit of laughing in
the face of tragedy and trauma.

I'd inherited his most prized possession. The pistol.
Not his daughter. Indians might have a chief running
things. Then a council, of course. But every family, clan,
nation, has a matriarchy at its root. His little girl wasn't
his. She was her own woman. If I was lucky enough,
she'd call me her man. Her closest cousin likes me. Her
dad did, too. The aunties were hot and cold, as far as I
could tell. Though, what everyone thought of me wasn't
exactly what mattered most on the day myself and five
others carried the old man to the spot where he'd be
planted from here on out.

It turns out they don't lower the dead into the dirt
anymore with the family still there out of fear of folks
flopping themselves on top of the casket. Caskets will
flip open sometimes, and the dearly departed will spill
out. Or, with their desperate loved one straddling them,
their stitches will let loose and their insides will spill out,

and then the one who did the belly flop atop the casket is covered with insides and innards. The other example of why they don't do so involves how some five-foot auntie could try to ride the casket down into the grave and couldn't climb out of a six-foot-hole once they calmed down enough to realize what they've gotten themselves into. I, too, learned how gravediggers are both chatty and simultaneously cluelessly callous. Who could blame them, though? Those they work with are closemouthed and soulless, as a rule.

Once we left the cemetery, and the number of folks who'd gathered to grieve split in half, I sat on the love-seat with one of the aunties who looked about the right age to be a sister to the old man. I didn't ask her any questions. I sat and listened to the commentary coming from her lips and let go a laugh when there was no more keeping my eavesdropping secret. I listened to the old woman comment to herself about this person, and that one for I-don't-know-how-long. Until I began to relearn names, at least. Eventually, Elise looked over to see me and the old lady leaning in toward one another, laughing at the room around us, and left us to our fuckery.

I don't know how long we sat for, but I do remember how our conversation came to an end. One of Elise's cousins butted in saying, "You a cop?"

"Huh?" I said, surprised at his sudden company. "Ah, hello. Ah. No, I am not a cop."

"Elise told me you're BIA, like, not even two minutes ago," he said, pointing back over his shoulder toward the kitchen.

I shook my head and told him, "I work as a Bail Enforcement Agent."

"That's what I asked, B—I—"

The old lady cut him off laughing as did everyone else who was now listening.

"Stop acting like you finally fricking learned how to spell. Auntie doesn't give money for good grades anymore. You're too late." Elise said to him, barking from one room into the next across the congregation of cousins and aunties and uncles. "You're stupid. It's embarrassing."

"It's okay, Elise," I said.

"No, it's not. He's trying to get all tough with you."

"Look," I said, making sure I had her cousin's attention once again. "I am a Bail Enforcement Agent. Enforcement starts with an E, not an I. Okay? I'm not BIA."

He narrowed his eyes. I could see the wheels turning inside his noggin, so I elaborated some more for him. "Look," I said and wiped my mouth to hide my smile. A smirk, really. "Fugitive Recovery Agent, is that better? Make any more sense to you?"

"What do you do, though?" he said, waving his hands mockingly.

"When somebody misses court and skips out on their bond, I track them down."

"Oh, cool," he said, "So, you're like a real, live Indian tracker."

"You're stupid," Elise yelled over the tops of everyone's heads. "He's a fricking bounty hunter, dumbass."

His eyes widened. "Badass!" he said so loud I couldn't help but close my eyes, turn my head, and wish I could close my ears, too. He sat across from the old lady and me, leaned in, and stared. His lips didn't budge.

Someone said something about him having a crush on me. Someone else said something else about him wanting to partner up with me and become a bounty hunter his own self, and he chimed in and said, "Yeah, I want to be a bounty hunter, too."

I swatted the idea away by saying, "The money isn't that great, and splitting it down the middle would make it nowhere near worth it."

"C'mon, I've seen those posters up at the post office: wanted by the FBI, one-million dollars and all that."

"That's different," I say. "That's for folks who're successfully evading the FBI."

"Then what do you do?" he asked again.

I didn't answer or attempt to. Instead, I dropped my head and carefully and thoroughly examined the square foot of the carpet between my feet.

A handful of minutes passed by before I felt a finger tap on the nape of my neck. I looked up to see Elise standing between her cousin and me. "Hey," she said. "Take me somewhere."

"Where do you want to go?"

"I don't know. Anywhere. I am all dressed up. Auntie'll kick everybody out when she's ready to go home, won't you?"

"Sure will," the old lady said, clamped her lips shut and let out a yawn through her nose, signaling it wouldn't be much longer before she did just that.

26

I TURNED OVER the engine and asked, "All right, where are we going?"

"I don't know, anywhere," Elise answered. "Screw it, let's go bowling."

I looked down toward the floor mat on the passenger side and asked, "In those shoes?"

"They give you bowling shoes, ya nerd," Elise said, and I let the car roll back out into the street.

"Which direction?" I asked.

"North of town, toward the tollway." She answered.

The drive over was quiet, mostly. I laughed, chortled, I guess, is more accurate. "You know, we're going to look entirely out of place at a bowling alley."

"No, not really," she said, correcting me. "It's dark as crap in there. They have music thumping and black lights everywhere. It's as close to a nightclub as we got."

"No valet?" I said, pulling into the parking lot. "What kind of nightclub is this?"

"Lawson's finest," Elise said.

Inside was as she said: music so loud you had to lean in inches from someone's ear to talk, adding a whole new level of intimacy to bowling I'd never before known. The place was big, considering. About two dozen lanes, maybe more.

Our first game wasn't anything special. Both she and I barely broke a hundred. That'll probably change the more I tell this story. We called it a warm-up game, asked our waitress for another round of drinks, set up another ten frames.

"I'm going to go to the bathroom," Elise said. "Why don't you bowl first this time?"

I nodded, and she bent over, pressed her lips to my forehead midstride.

My ball was oily and spun this way and that—all over the lane—and ended up striking the pins on the far left-hand side, knocking down a little less than half. I dried my fingertips with the air blowing from the ball return and heard her yell my name right as my ball got birthed back into my waiting hands. I turned around so fast and leaned in to listen to what she was saying so excitedly over and over again that we headbutted one another.

"What?" I said after making sure she was okay, bumped head and all.

She placed a hand on each of my shoulders, leaned in, and said, "Eric, Eric Drumgoole…Junior…just walked into the men's room."

I stood up straight and looked over her right shoulder toward the restrooms, "I shit you not," she said, shaking her head.

I took her for serious and made my way to the restrooms to see for myself without bothering to put my ball back down.

Inside the men's room, there stood one sink and one stall and one urinal that goes all the way to the floor and allows your piss to splash all over your shoes and pant legs. Sitting in the stall was someone wearing jeans and street shoes. They were either coming or going. I say that because they were either yet to change into their bowling shoes or had already changed out of them and decided to take a dump before hitting the road.

A courtesy flush was in order, but I didn't let myself get too concerned with how bad the bathroom stank because of him. Instead, I power walked over toward the stall and tugged at the handle.

"Somebody's in here, man," a voice said, sounding startled. Between the crack in the door and the frame, I caught a sliver of his face, enough to know it was indeed him.

"Sorry," I said. "Are you almost done? I think I am going to crap my pants, man."

"Yeah, gimme a second."

I rocked my feet back and forth, back and forth, making him think my pants would explode at any second.

"Hold on, man, don't shit your britches. I'm wiping, okay."

I would like to thank the academy.

I stepped a few feet back and turned the deadbolt as he flushed. Right when the latch on the stall door clicked open, I volleyed the bowling ball into the door with everything I had and followed right behind it. I launched myself into the door with my right knee leading the way and my hands covering my face.

Junior didn't make a sound. Not one that could be heard over the collapse of the door or the bowling ball wandering its way over the tile floor toward the sink behind me or the spreading pool of water that came from the ceramic tank formerly situated on the back of the toilet.

It looked like the inside of the door hit him directly in the forehead between the eyebrows when the bowling ball crashed into the outer aluminum panel. His nose looked knocked to the side. His teeth looked loosened, too. He was, for the time being, what emergency medical technicians refer to as unresponsive.

Without giving too much detail, I told Elise I needed her to go into my trunk and get the bag from Candy's Toy Box and bring it into the men's room. Then I pulled the out-of-order sign out of the custodian's room and waited.

"Holy shit," Elise said as soon as I let her inside the bathroom.

"Help me dress him," is all I said back.

When a woman strolls out of the men's room leading a man by a chain and metal pinch dog collar, everyone who takes their eyes off their bowling lane might stare, but no one considers stopping her from leaving. Not when said man is wearing a leather hood along with a vintage-looking straitjacket, and she's wearing a black pencil dress and a pair of high heels with hair and makeup done in a fashion sure to call to mind one of the simply irresistible women from the Robert Palmer music video.

Mister Eric Delvin Drumgoole Junior shuffled his feet as far as the ankle chain would allow, almost two-stepping along with the music synced with the laser lights in the bowling alley.

I wish I could have watched the spectacle, but the car needed to be brought as close to the front doors as possible.

"Drive safe," is all she said when I dropped her off in front of her house.

I idled on the shoulder while she skirted her way around the hood of the Sunbird, leaned in my window, kissed my forehead. "Later," she said.

"Later," I repeated and watched her tread up the driveway, onto the front porch, unlock the front door, flick on the front yard light, which set the charcoal-stained cement of the driveway aglow.

Seven coyotes—in various states of bloat and decomposition—is what I counted once I started keeping track; once it struck me how there was more lying alongside the highway than I'd ever seen upon any one stretch of road. They damn near served as mile markers. And with them, all splayed out—with their population so thinned out—I wondered what would become of the rest of the roadkill. Flies can only do so much. Would the other coyotes take care of them? And for that matter, what does it take for a coyote to become a cannibal? How hungry does one have to get before dog-eat-dog becomes literal? I'd bet crows are too jumpy to dig into one, no matter how bloated and alluring the bouquet. I bet the turkey vultures will pick up the slack—along with the eagles.

Anything can have happened in Oklahoma. Practically everything has. Someone a lot smarter than me said that once. I'll be damned if I can remember who.

27

OVERDRIVING CAUSES one to be equally dangerous behind the wheel as a drunk. Things blindside you while you're flirting with Mister Sandman and send a shot of adrenaline straight to your heart or colon or the medulla oblongata in the back of the brain. I could not say with any real authority how that particular chemical works in the body. Though I do know if you blink a bit too long and get nudged awake by the rumble strips running along the shoulder of the road, that'll do a better job of waking you than any yellowjackets for sale at any truck stop—or anything else you can find being peddled in the parking lot.

I also know the average American black bear weighs between two hundred to five hundred pounds. So, when you come upon a curve in the road and see one saunter through the grassy median, it's a sight worthy of your undivided attention.

If you're smart, you'll put your hands at ten and two and get ready for evasive maneuvers.

The reason I say this is that my mother once played a game of chicken with a bear on the highway and lost.

Her Olds Omega rolled down a ravine and came to a halt after it wedged itself between two pine trees. The chrome-plated latch on the moonroof tore the top of her head open like the leather stretched across a baseball, but no bones were broken. None of the windows shattered either or even spiderwebbed. Fortunately, she kept what I'll call a tire-thumper tucked under her driver's seat. It was a sort of a miniature wooden baseball bat she spun on a lathe back in her high school woodshop class. For extra credit, she'd countersunk a threaded lead weight on the inside. That's how she got out through the back window and shuffled her way a half-mile down the highway to the closest house where she asked if she couldn't use the bathroom to clean herself up somewhat and maybe use the telephone.

An ambulance pulled into the driveway by the time she came back out of the bathroom. She was puzzled as to why her hair was wet. She was a redhead, but not blood red.

Shock does that.

Yet when the curve in the road unfurled, things became less of a blur, and it wasn't a bear at all, but three black dogs. At seventy-something miles-an-hour, they looked like littermates to me. I'd guess they were black Labs mixed with something with a broader chest. Maybe English Labs, now that I think about it. They were tearing into a felled deer. Well, one was watching while the other two feasted. They took turns, I'd guess, at least.

Three black dogs, like something out of a fairy tale. But not one that ends with a happily ever after.

Coming out of that curve, my eyes lingered on the trio a little longer than I should have allowed. I couldn't help but notice how I'd failed to unwind the steering wheel enough to keep within the white and yellow lines of the highway's slow lane. The radials made a sound of protest reminding me of running a dried brick of sharp cheddar across a cheese grater. Elise shot up in her seat, snapped her head to the right, looked down into the looming ditch then over toward me in the driver's seat, and said, "You want me to drive?"

The gimp was gone from the back seat, settled into a holding cell where he'd stay until the judge was ready to deal with him that coming Monday morning.

For Elise and me, *later* came sooner rather than later. Love does that.

"Find someplace to pull off," she said through a yawn, and I coasted us down an exit another mile down the road. The city sidewalks seemed long since rolled up, but there was one building that looked like it still supported life. The place looked windowless. That's to say the only light that shone in the parking lot lit the last few spots closest to the front door, but there wasn't one beer sign seen fizzling behind a single pane of glass. The parking lot was a mowed field nestled up against the backside of a cornfield, giving the whole place an if-you-build-it-they-will-come kind of charm. The wall facing the freeway read BIKER FRIENDLY. BYOB adorned the cinder blocks stretched across the archway. Stenciled beneath that was NO ONE UNDER 21.

"Moe, why're we at…*The Outhouse*," Elise asked and swallowed a stifled snicker.

"I have to pee," I said, prying the steel door away from the frame, allowing her to step out of the buggy early evening autumn weather before I did.

"I have a feeling we are not in Kansas anymore," Elise said while her eyeballs blinked rapid-fire, trying to process the oddity around her—a strip club without any live nude girls in sight.

"Nope," I said, angling an arm over her left shoulder to draw her attention toward a vinyl sign I saw hanging over the bar that explained why we had to pay an extra five bucks each at the door. We'd slogged into the middle of The Saturday Night Midget Wrestling Show. "We're in the land of the little people now," I said and turned on my heel, headed toward the men's room, left Elise to find us a table as close to ringside as feasible.

28

Any asshole who thinks they can successfully step into a ring with a wrestler, Thai fighter, boxer, or onto the field with any other trained athlete, and do what they do, is just that: an asshole. That includes exotic dancers, cheerleaders, rodeo clowns, bull and bronc riders, as well as luchadores and *wrasslers*. And said asshole deserves any ass-kicking and accompanying heckling coming their way.

It's better than cable T.V. for those sitting ringside.

Take Exhibit A, who I'll call the Rick Flair of asinine spectators amongst what grew into a standing-room-only audience. He wouldn't close his mouth for more than a fistful of seconds all night long and presented himself ringside without hesitation when the announcer quieted the crowd to let us know the challenger for the evening's main event had taken ill, and, since the night was still young, they were wondering whether someone from the crowd might have it in them to take on their champion.

Ole fucknoggin even grabbed a feather boa from one of the ring card girls and draped it over his shoulders before he slithered between the ropes and on into the ring.

He peacocked his way around the ring, strutted beneath the beauty lights, took victory laps before the match ever began. Before his third lap around the ring, another ring card girl entered with a clipboard in hand. The announcer asked the enthusiastic gentleman if he wouldn't sign a form. His question was a simple one, "what for?"

"In case of bodily injury," the announcer said.

He answered back with a crooked smile and a shake of his head and put pen to paper without blinking his eyes or even squinting to see exactly what the glowing white form entailed. Then when he lifted his hand away from the clipboard, Lil Hank shot beneath the bottom rope and forced his head and feet trade places.

John Lee Hooker's *Boom Boom* rang out from the speakers and Lil Hank screamed, "You're in my house!" almost echoing John Lee as he finished the first verse.

The challenger rolled onto his back and looked up from the faceplant he'd made onto the mat, stupefied.

Pride comes before the fall.

Lil Hank wore cowboy boots, Wranglers, a black leather vest, a blood-red dew rag to keep the sweat out of his eyes, a horseshoe mustache, and a bald head. Nothing for anyone taller than him to grab onto, in other words.

Pain filled the challenger's eyes, made them glisten, and he snarled, humiliated beyond imagination. Lil Hank saw this and beamed—as did I—along with everyone else close enough to see or sober enough to give their undivided attention.

Before the challenger could get back to his feet, Lil Hank exploded into his gut like a cannonball shot close range at a strongman in a freakshow back when that equated quality entertainment—except the challenger didn't stand his ground and shake it off. Instead, he folded in two before he found himself splayed out once more on the mat with Lil Hank towering over him.

The challenger tried to sit up but made that face everyone makes when they are not entirely certain if they let go of a fart or shit themselves a teensy bit. It's the same face you might make when you're drunk, feeling pretty good—numb almost—and then the fog lifts, and the broken rib clears its throat to make sure you're listening for the next thing to roll off its tongue.

When that sort of pain washes over a person, there's nausea, of course, but things move in slow motion, too. Most say it's like they feel drunk. But if you are drunk and going through something similar, it's more of an out-of-body experience, so you sit back and watch the show with the rest of the audience, rather than react.

Lil Hank sailing from the top rope through the smoky air of The Outhouse, parting the clouds as he went, was a majestic sight to see. That's not to forget the folding chair he held overhead and used as a makeshift parachute meant to break his fall and knock the challenger senseless so he could pin him to the mat with ease and have the whole place take part in the ten-count along with the miniature referee.

Fun for the whole family.

Of course, the challenger kicked his legs at the last second and managed to wriggle his shoulders off the mat right around the same time the ref slapped his hand down for the ninth time, so we were going to get our money's worth after all.

29

NOT A SINGLE INSTANCE of anything good in the history of the spoken word ever came from someone beginning a sentence with a hushed, "Don't look now, but…" but that is what Elise leaned in and hollered into my ear: "Don't look now, but this place is crawling with Basterds."

She was referring to the motorcycle brethren who beat and hospitalized me and meant to send my last skip trace to an early and unmarked grave. BIKER FRIENDLY as the wall so plainly stated when we approached from the highway. But with her lips and breath brushing my earlobe, the words on her tongue left me with a mix of emotions akin to the tingle Mary Jane Watson sent down through Spiderman's short hairs.

"Yeah," I said, annunciating at my very finest for the sake of clarity, so I would not have to repeat what was coming next: "This place is wall-to-wall assholes. That is what happens when the circus comes to town, everyone wants to watch the freakshow."

"No," she said. "There's a giant-ass Basterds patch painted on the back wall in the ladies' room."

"Oh," I said and gave her my full attention, neglecting

to close my mouth all the way when I was done talking. She rolled her eyes toward the front door, took hold of my wrist to lead the way out, and I did not resist her charms.

"You want to drive a while?" I said.

"Yeah, sure," she said, taking the keys in her hand and trotting off toward my Pontiac faster than I.

Broiling exhaust burrowed its way through the darkened, damp night air and led me to where Elise waited in the car. I saw the thermostat was warmed when I sat and leaned back to toss a handful of plug wires down onto the rear floorboards.

"What...did you do?"

"The same thing I used to do when my mom was too drunk to drive but wouldn't give up her keys," I said as I turned back around to face forward and buckle in. "Drive, please."

She put it in gear, crawled across the parking lot, eased out onto the highway. Only then did she turn on the headlights and assume her role as a getaway driver.

"There wasn't anybody watching the bikes?" she said, swiveling her head to check the trio of mirrors after merging off the on-ramp and into the slow lane.

"Nope, who is dumb enough to monkey with their bikes outside of their clubhouse? And they were snuggled against one another in a nice little row, so I didn't have to go hunting."

"You're an idiot, Moe."

"I love you, too," I said. She didn't say anything back to me, but I could hear her smile. Or maybe I was imagining her face radiating heat when she blushed, and it was just the defroster warming up the windshield. "Cruise control will save on gas," I said, settling into my headrest and smiling at the windshield with eyes closed.

"What's on the stereo?" Elise asked before I made my way to Lalaland.

"Hah," I let go a laugh and thought for a second. "On one station there's a beleaguered preacher, a sing-song priest on another, followed by a joyous preacher, and I remember an angry preacher somewhere on the dial, too. Oh, and the farm report. The station from the college is playing techno. Listen to that for too long, and it'll hypnotize you—we'll wake in either the ditch or the next world."

30

AN AMERICAN BISON'S eyeballs do reflect light—if they're looking in the direction of oncoming traffic, that is—the same as a deer or a dog caught in a set of headlights. It's a good thing, too, since a mature male can tip the scales at a little over a ton. The moose is the only thing I have ever heard that doesn't reflect light. Maybe that's because they stand ten feet off the ground, and most headlights sit around two feet off the road, four and a half—max— if it's a lifted truck.

The American Bison has two speeds: stampede and stroll. They are also capable of standing still. Dead stop, as some call it. They'll do that while grazing or emptying their bladder or evacuating their large intestines, but not while they sleep. They don't always roam the prairie surprisingly enough either. Highways have much to be desired when the ground gets too soft.

I think astrology is a load of horseshit. Taurus doesn't look like a bull at all. It looks a lot like a tuning fork. The bear that has the big dipper for a rump and tail looks like a preschooler drew a stick figure dog. A fox I could see, more so, with the pointy nose and ears laid back. But not a bear.

It took me a while to realize I was staring at stars. I didn't think stars flickered the way they were. Before that, it was as black as I imagine the inside of a coffin to be once the lid is closed and six feet of soil gets shoveled on top. I blinked automatically or subconsciously to get the blood and diced up tiny cubes of glass away from my eyes. The moonlight sparkled through the edges of what was left of the windshield, letting me know I was not ejected from the vehicle. The dash and glove box moved so near my chest, I could have used it for a chin rest had my seatbelt not locked up and lashed me to my seat without an inch of wiggle room.

I thought I heard the radiator gurgling.

The hood peeled off toward the driver's side, so I had an unobstructed view of the radiator. It was shoved into the fan and tamped onto the front of the engine block like the soft aluminum it was. Beyond all that mess, I saw the wild-eyed expression of a buffalo staring back at me. The bumper looked embedded in its side, and its breath exhaled through a gill that came courtesy of its loitering along a quiet and curvy stretch of State Highway 99 during the early morning hours.

Elise was worse off.

I undid my seatbelt to reach over and close her eyes. When I leaned her way, the belt slid off my left shoulder, and gravity slunk my arm down between the seat and door. That's to say, I had no control over it. I didn't know it had dislocated. It didn't hurt. I wouldn't call it numb, either.

Just because, I put two fingers alongside her windpipe, hoping to feel even the slightest throb of a pulse.

When I did, I saw how she had all the rigidity of a soaking-wet ragdoll. She put her head on her right shoulder, pinching my palm in between in doing so.

There's a thick foggy area between touching someone to check for signs of life and the dead moving and touching you. It's not something you can prepare yourself for, and knee jerk is the only honest way to categorize what happens after. To say I shot out of my seat and onto the blacktop might be a sloppy way of describing it, but when such a realization kicks you in the gut so hard that you can't figure out if you are going to throw up or soil yourself, sometimes you just stand there quietly and bleed.

Elise was married to the steering wheel. That's to say, it was the end of our love story.

31

"**ARE YOU TRYING** to tell me if I send a deputy ten miles up the road, he's going to radio back about how there's a turquoise Pontiac with a dead buffalo for a hood ornament, and your girlfriend, also dead, behind the steering wheel?"

I cast my eyes down to my lap and interlaced my fingers, pantomimed, flapped them as best I could to call attention to them, "More like mushed into than behind," I said back to the lieutenant. "I counted ten mileposts. Maybe a few more. My head doesn't feel the best."

"Well, why not, Sherlock? Did you walk by any glass storefronts before I flagged you down? The folks who called us said they thought a zombie had crawled up out of the grave and came to town to wreak who knows what sort of hell. You really should thank them if you get the chance. Adrenaline has you so hopped on autopilot you might have merged back on the highway, headed to Tulsa. Traffic isn't so thin down there," he said, turning and looking south. "Do you mind telling me where you were walking on such a beautiful Sunday morning?"

"Toward some church bells."

"You need a doctor's help. Talk to Jesus some other time."

"Don't doctors go to church?"

"Let the boys in the ambulance take you to get patched up. Hmm, what say you? That shoulder looks mangled. Out of socket, separated, something. You should see it."

I rolled my eyes down and to the right, said, "Neck's too stiff for that at the moment."

"Yeah," he said, closing his notebook, tucking it into the breast pocket behind his badge. "I could not wager why," he added, giving the EMT a head nod.

I squinted my best to read his badge number: 521. I liked those odds—the odds of remembering those three digits versus his rank and name were all the more likely, given my fuzzy demeanor. "Nighty night," I said, "Deputy Vegas," letting the paramedic ease me back onto the gurney. I could already feel the creeping cold coursing its way up my arm.

"Vegas?" he said, confused and looked down at his nameplate and back at me, which made me chuckle, then cough. Rinse, lather, repeat. Cops don't like getting laughed at, but it's hard to get too mad at the freshly concussed.

The IHS staff treated me for said concussion after a trip to the radiology department. They treated me for a separated shoulder, as well, both of which would heal on their own with enough rest, relaxation, and Fentanyl, an analgesic, which I pronounced *anal-geese-sick* when the doctor first handed me the vat of a bottle.

"It's for around the clock pain management," the doctor said.

"Hell of a lot of them in here," I replied and shook the bottle, which did not rattle as much as one might expect.

"And two refills," I said after scanning the label again. The bottle was big enough to kill a buffalo, had it not already met an untimely end.

"Flush them if you don't need them. Or sell them, whatever you do with them after you leave here is beyond my control."

"That's all right. I have a job. Fugitive Recovery Agent," I said, pocketing the pills.

"With one good arm and no vehicle? Good luck seeing much cash flow that way."

"I wasn't aware pain pills were the new wampum in Indian country."

"Yeah, well, hey, don't drink with those either. Nurse'll walk you out in a minute or so," the doctor said and disappeared, pulling my curtain closed so I could change back into the clothes I'd worn the night before, blood and salt-stained from being sweat-soaked. I smelled like a farm animal or a farmhand. Or a slaughterhouse, or, maybe, a dead buffalo.

Osage Laundry is a straight shot from the Indian Health Center. Less than a block away to get my clothes clean. My shirt, at least. I wasn't about to drop my pants and leisurely loiter around the laundromat like it was my living room.

It turns out the town is so small that it's one of those places no one bothers to lock either their front doors or car door, and where a woman will leave her husband's wash unattended while they attend Sunday services—and brunch. God bless them.

Two signs hung inside the laundromat. One, which swayed over the rumbling washing machines, read WASH OILY CLOTHES HERE. I couldn't tell whether they meant the one washer directly beneath the sign in the middle of the bank of wash machines or the entire eclectic collection of washers they'd managed to amass inside the tiny laundromat. It didn't look like the kind of place where one would wash their Sunday best.

The other sign said, SMILE! YOU ARE ON CAMERA. Above that, attached to the wall with double-stick tape, was a fake surveillance camera—otherwise known as a psychological deterrent. This one didn't even have a battery-operated red light to look like the real deal. There wasn't even a piece of coax coming out of the backside that whoever would have to tuck inside the ceiling tiles so it didn't dangle and give up the ruse. That same someone, whomever the proprietor might be, stenciled NO SMOKING onto all four canary-yellow walls with fire-engine red spray paint. The glowing walls, along with the lingering scent of crude oil, mingling with cow shit and dryer sheets exceeded the Fentanyl the doctor gave me to turn my five senses into fog lights.

I'm no thief. Indians trade. I pulled off my shirt and tossed it into a basket of dirty clothes yet to get spun around a washer before I went browsing through a dryer full of clothing that had ended its cycle and cooled off somewhat. The pants I found I had to cuff, but I'd need a belt, too, if I didn't want to walk around with my hands stuffed into my pockets so they could serve as suspenders. Fresh warm socks are always a nice thing to slide on, but I stayed with my own underwear. There's no way I'd slip into someone else's skivvies, clean, starched, pressed, or otherwise.

Osage Laundry was the first building after the first streetlight on the north end of town, or it sat right before the last streetlight on the north edge of town, depending on your direction of travel. For that reason, I turned south and walked a half a dozen or so blocks to Main Street.

Some things are easily missed while driving versus walking. The smell of a restaurant kitchen tucked down a side street with no real signage to speak of as a means of keeping their location as secretive as possible in the hopes of detracting the interest of any tourists who might wander off the beaten path, for instance. Another hint you should take your appetite elsewhere is a hand-written sign next to the hostess stand that reads LOCAL CHECKS ONLY. At least that is something I have learned to watch for in my travels. Of course, exceptions exist for every rule. Another thing life has taught me is not to gaze down any darkened or dead-end alleyways.

Alleyways can house any number of boogiemen if cinema has taught me anything. But when hymns are trickling out an alley and onto Main Street rather than used oil or a drunken hobo's morning piss stream, it's worthy of further investigation.

This particular alley dead-ended at a monstrosity of a stage built out of past-their-prime railroad ties. As were the two dozen mirrored rows of backless pews. The preacher spoke no louder than one would if they sat across the table at a diner between the breakfast and lunch rush. Yet, his voice crept along the entire length of both brick walls. All in attendance heard his words whether they sat up front or in the very back, giving the alleyway a Sermon-on-the-Mount kind of feel, which compelled me to plop my ass cheeks down in the second to the last row.

I mumbled along with those to the left, right, back, and front of me, but caught on by the third or fourth time the chorus came around.

The line to take communion was slow-going. I'm not an active Christian by any means, but I know how to take orders, camouflage myself, act uniformly with those around me. It's called soldiering in the Army. It's the same as being one of the Lord's sheep come Sunday morning.

The little square of bread was the first thing to enter my stomach since the previous afternoon. It did little more than make my gut growl. The gentlemen who had the job of splashing the wine across every communer's tongue must have been a fixture at his fraternity keggers. He knew the precise angle to tilt that chalice so you wouldn't choke or even need to swallow. He could pour it right down my throat. And did. I'd swear I committed the involuntary sinful act of gluttony while taking communion. I, too, would testify that the Savior's blood was clotted. Chunky.

I wouldn't bother to wager whether my picking out a new outfit from the laundromat had been forgiven courtesy of my one act of congregation. Though, I sat there in the pew along with a peppering of elderly women once the service came to an end. It's not as if I wanted to converse with the Lord in private, but my legs would not do as asked.

Luckily, loitering in an outdoor church isn't against any enforceable laws.

32

"G'AFTERNOON, MOSES," I heard a vaguely familiar voice say over the hum of all-terrain tires lunging along a neglected stretch of highway. "I got to worrying. You breathe all kinds of shallow when you're out of it, you know that?"

To talk proved difficult for reasons I was not expecting. The side of my face was stuck to the rear passenger-side window of a patrol car as though someone had licked my cheek and whipped my head into the window in the hopes it would stick like it was something they'd pulled out of the bottom of a cereal box. My neck was at what I would call an unnatural angle. I tried to put my left palm on the seat to sit back, but little did I know, my left wrist was handcuffed to my right one. I wound up yanking my arm out of the sling and shot up straight, fell forward, mashed my face against the cage separating the backseat from the front when the pain floated from my shoulder straight to my brainstem, "How-ow-ow-ow!"

"How? Moses, I thought you people didn't say that except in the movies?"

"Let my people go," I said, doing my best to blink

away the tears welling in my eyes while staring down at my cuffed wrists.

"Deputy Vegas?" I asked without moving anything other than my lower jaw, not wanting to invite any more pain or agony.

"How do you like them apples? Or was it *odds* you said earlier to me in the ambulance? I figured we'd cross paths again."

"521 odds. It was *odds*."

"And it's Lieutenant Wair, not Deputy Vegas."

"Wire?"

"No, stomp on the *W* when you say it. It's *liar* but with a *W* starting off."

"Liar, huh?"

"Yep, and now it's time for some truth-telling. I have some questions," he said, hoisting an evidence bag up toward the headliner of the cruiser. "Got your wallet here, a shitload of cash—we'll circle back to that—and enough pills to sedate a few dozen folks for a holiday weekend. I dare say it's not worth charging you with attempting to distribute, since I found you outside your mind, putting every preacher in town to shame. We can call that disorderly conduct easily enough, and it's a far lesser charge and considerably easier for me to prove. I'd lock you up, but you need to dry out. I don't want to listen to your clamoring while I am at my desk," he said, peering at me through the rearview mirror. "I can understand you being distraught with your girlfriend and the wreck, et cetera. But the cash. Let's chit chat about the cash, shall we? We'll be on the road for a while. Let's come clean about that little mystery, at least."

"The cash is mine. It's my twenty percent. What's left."

"What sort of job did you do to garner that sort of

cash? For that matter, what makes you so brave as to walk around with that in your wallet?"

"Where're we headed? Fewer houses are zipping by now."

"County detox center in Bartlesville. We don't have one, and the Osage says you're not theirs."

"I'm not. I'm Ho-Chunk."

"You getting sick back there? Goddammit!"

"What?"

"Blow chunks. Are you about to blow chunks in my cruiser?" the lieutenant said, already slowing down and undoing his seatbelt. "Tell me, damn it so that I can pull off onto the shoulder. I do not want to clean up my car again already."

"No," I said and slapped my back against the hard plastic of the seat behind me. "I am Ho-Chunk. Wisconsin, you know?"

"No. No, I don't. What the hell are you doing down here?"

"Playing chicken with buffalo," I said to myself, laughing and closed my eyes.

"Speak up."

I cleared my throat with such force I felt a pinch, and I swallowed it down, too, knowing better than to spit on a cop's floor, "I'm a bail bonds recovery agent."

"Shit. You one of Ephrem's guys?"

"Never heard of her," I said and batted my eyes while I pulled the smuggest look I could in case the lieutenant was looking my way.

"Shit. Hell, I'm going turn around up here. You like barbeque?"

"Are you paying?"

"Absolutely," he said, lifting the evidence bag back up

into the air again. "Hey, I've already seen you're wad."

"It's feast or famine with my profession," I interjected.

"I vote we feast," he said, smiling into the rearview mirror the way a dog would when it gets to sneak a mouthful of fresh cat shit from the litter box.

33

THE PIG SHACK sat caddy-corner from Osage Laundry—within eyeshot of the scene of the crime. Lieutenant Wiar sat with his back to the laundromat, and I did all I could to not glance at it over his shoulder too often. I didn't want to allude to any degree of guilt of any crime, if at all possible.

"Eat," he said. "That'll fix a few of your problems."

I kept chewing, kept listening. Oklahoma barbecue was different than Kansas City-style. Not better, or worse. Different. Dry, but that's why there's Sweet tea.

"The pain doc set you up with a 90-day supply of Fentanyl atop whatever he put in the saline drip to ease your shoulder pain and whatever else you injured, and then you went to that alley church with that goof-ass preacher. That's your day thus far?"

"Since I saw you last, yes. I woke up in the back of a cop car. There's that."

"You were blacked out, but never unconscious, really."

"Okay," I said.

"You know, that preacher, he makes his own communion wine?"

"Oh?"

The lieutenant laughed at a joke only he was aware of and asked, "Ever heard of sour mash?"

"Whiskey?"

"Yeah, you need to make sour mash to make whiskey. That's what they boil and distill. If you ever make it to Tennessee, take a tour of Lynchburg. It's pretty impressive. Worth the price of admission."

"All right."

"Anyway. For wine, there's the same thing, but it's called must or mustum. Then they do whatever to it and make wine. But if they don't turn the must into wine, then it keeps right on fermenting, tastes like rotten fruit. But that preacher says communion shouldn't be a pleasurable experience in the first place. The stuff ends up being somewhere between twenty-three and twenty-five percent alcohol, the way he tells it. I am not sure of the proof. Up there, I'd guess. Now, mix that with the party pack of pain meds you got, and you're setting off into orbit."

"And I become a walking, talking *Sunday Morning Coming Down*," I added.

"And Bingo was his name-o," the lieutenant said in a singsong voice. "Pass me a paper towel if you would please."

"We finish up here, I'll ride you out to the Cavalcade Inn. It's not a bragging point for the town, but if you're a soldier, you've slept in worse accommodations."

"I appreciate that."

"What else?" he said to himself. "Your car is in the salvage yard on the north end of town. I'd clean it out before someone else does just that for you. They'll probably buy it off you for scrap, part-out what they can."

I nodded to let him know I was considering all he had to say.

"Your girlfriend's mother's family, they've been contacted. A few of them still live around here," he added while spinning a finger overhead, meaning inside the three-square miles of the town around us.

I shook my head at all of that, kept chewing through some burnt ends, broke my silence finally by saying, "We were coming to visit," to the last part.

"The best advice I can offer right now is to clean out your car once you're feeling more like yourself, but don't let them talk you into buying anything off the lemon lot they got out there. Trust me on that one. Mourn your girlfriend and that automobile of yours in your own way. Do me a favor, please, and deadbolt yourself into your hotel room if you're thinking about drinking while on them pills. I'd also advise that you, please, don't open the door at that place unless someone has dropped you a line letting you know they are coming to visit beforehand."

"I can scrap."

"No, you can't. You couldn't even wipe your ass and blow your nose at the same time right now."

"You got me on that one."

"I'll let your girlfriend's family know where you are staying. The funeral should be in a few more days here. I can pick you up or tell whatever deputy is going to lead the procession to grab you on the way."

I nodded again while swallowing more than I could chew.

34

PAWHUSKA PULL-A-PART & SALVAGE sits three blocks west of
the Osage Indian Baptist Church. After we passed the
salvage yard, we had another four blocks to drive until
we passed beneath the archway marking the entrance to
the city cemetery. I sat in front of the patrol car this time.

I didn't bother to make myself known or go out of
my way to call attention to my presence at the visitation,
or the wake. I couldn't say why with any agency. I let
myself imagine it would wind up feeling a lot like hi and
goodbye all in one breath. So I held my tongue, held my
breath, did not part my lips one time that I can recall.

Still, I felt like the woman in the long black veil.
Though, I knew I was nothing more than the elephant
in the room. No one came over to me to shake my hand,
slap my shoulder, say sorry. What do you say to the guy
who damn near died alongside the person who did? I
said goodbye to Elise when I closed her eyes and again
when they forklifted my Pontiac into the crusher so they
could pay me by the pound for the aluminum and steel
by which they would glean its worth.

Fireman cut the steering wheel off the steering

column at the dash. I took note of that when I cleaned out the trunk and gave the insides a quick once over. It's something I could have done without seeing. It wasn't on the floorboard or tossed into the backseat. Realizing that, my mind snapped back to her closed casket, and I knew it, too, rest inside.

Elise's aunties and uncles and cousins were laughing and talking amongst each other, telling stories as storytellers do. All stories, if continued far enough, end in death, and he is no true storyteller who would keep that from you. That's Hemingway there, the king of cutting stories short.

35

WHEN WE FIRST MET, Lieutenant Wiar made mention of how he was a little worried I would merge back onto *Oklahoma 99* and walk my way down to Tulsa, where traffic wasn't so thin. *99* only goes so far south before you start heading back toward the middle of nowhere. But my thumb, as it turns out, can take me in any conceivable direction.

Hitchhiking isn't illegal in the state of Oklahoma, merely ill-advised. Outside of Hominy, a sign warns how HITCHHIKERS MAY BE ESCAPING INMATES. There are all sorts of things wrong with the verbiage of that sign. For one, there's nothing saying anything about not stopping and offering anyone a ride. Still, the road sign is yellow, not black and white, so it's merely a cautionary suggestion to passing motorists.

El Gordo Auto Sales sat between the Tulsa Greyhound Bus Station and a Cuban cuisine lunch counter that boasted the best Cuban sandwich in town. El Gordo should have had the tagline of "As-Is." That said, there was a 1982 Dodge Mirada for $5k, tax, title, and a topped-off tank. The 360 V8 is why he asked so much for such an aging and obscure automobile.

"Most are 225 slant sixes," the salesman said, popping the hood.

"So what?" I lobbed back, "it's still an automatic."

"Petty drove one," El Gordo said through the toothiest smile he could manage while still holding a conversation.

"Did he drive this one?"

"No, he did not."

"Good. Cause you're barking up the wrong tree. I was raised a David Pearson fan."

"No shit?" he said without blinking. He let the hood slam down and latch itself closed, defeated. I could almost see the hamster behind his sparkling eyes stumble and try its best to regain some traction.

It was absolute, unfiltered shit, what I had said to him. Auto racing was about as engaging to me as watching tennis on a 10" black and white T.V. with a busted antenna.

"How long," I asked, "has this automotive relic squatted on your lot?"

He sealed his lips and didn't offer an answer.

"How many miles has it been test-driven in that time?" I added.

"I'd have to check in my office," he said.

"Thirty-five hundred sounds fair, doesn't it?"

"Fair? Four sounds more like it to me if we are negotiating."

"Nope."

"No?"

"I mean, I'll need a set of new tires, right? which I'll buy from elsewhere *if* I buy this car off you. I couldn't ever get up to speed with the mismatched socks you slapped on her."

"The car tops out at 185."

"Not with dry-rotted sidewalls. Thirty miles an hour,

max. And what is that, Granny Smith Green?"

"My mechanic said it's called Sour Apple and would help it sell, make it look like the racecar it is."

"Racecar," I echoed. "Thirty-five hundred. That's all you'll get out of me. You can pull someone's pants down tomorrow over the price of that Plymouth Arrow pickup."

"Hell, I'm tired of us two standing around and tickling each other's ass. I'm ready to head home. My pens and paperwork are inside. How do you want to finance this?"

"Finance? No. I'll pay you cash in full today."

"Fuck me. Cash?"

"You are not my type. Besides—I just got out of a relationship."

"Breakups can be a real bitch, so can women. Sounds like yours took your car and left." I didn't answer. Instead, I let him lead the way into his malt shop turned used car dealership. I sat in the cracked-pleather chair facing his and swiveled my head to take in the glass walls that made up three-fourths of the place and said something concerning those in glass houses.

"Moses, while we are sitting, shuffling through these papers, I hope you don't mind, but I have to ask about the sling and the limp," he said and cast his eyes over my other shoulder to examine the clock on the wall. "Call me a curious cat. I just want to have something to tell my wife when I get home late."

"Please, call me Moe," I said and looked down at the sling, unfurled my fingers, coiled them back into a fist.

"Okay, Moe. Moses on the title, though, right?" he said, plunging his pointer finger down on top of the pile of papers.

"That's right," I said and ran my tongue between the

outside of my teeth and the inside of my lips, wanting to rid my mouth of the cotton feel. "My girlfriend ran a buffalo down with my car."

"Christ all Friday! Some ladies shouldn't drive, now should they? And that's how you screwed up your shoulder there? Boy, I'll tell you, seat belts cause more injuries than metal dashboards ever did as far as I am concerned. What about that limp you got?"

"I kicked the buffalo in the face until it was dead."

"You kicked a Buffalo to death? Beat it to death? Like punted it? Went for the extra point? On a one-ton American Bison?"

I didn't offer any clarification on the matter. I let El Gordo fill in the blanks in my backstory along with the tax, title, and registration.

"Well, hell, what did that innocent little buffalo ever do to you?" he asked, fishing for more conversation.

"Killed my girlfriend."

"I'll need you to sign this top one in triplicate if you could please," he said and mashed his teeth together to not let anything else slip out of his soundhole. I say soundhole simply because everything else about El Gordo's physicality matched that of a Mariachi Guitarrón.

The next morning, a burning question arose as to what I was still doing in Oklahoma. I am not so sure how long I pondered the pros and cons, but somehow my subconscious became convinced that given enough time, I could find the answer amidst the smoke floating above a smoldering Eggo. It was the closest I'd come to a vision quest in all my adult years courtesy of the Fentanyl gifted to me by the generous IHS medicine man.

Acknowledgments

I WANT TO THANK Ron Earl Phillips for pulling this book from the slush pile and being its first fan. To everyone who read this book—Penni Jones, Steph Post, Kelli Jo Ford, David Joy, Gabino Iglesias, Bonnie Jo Campbell, S.A. Cosby, Michael Farris Smith, Nick Kolakowski, Scott Phillips, Stephen Mack Jones, J. David Osborne, and Dr. Theo C. Van Alst Jr—thank you!

To everyone reading Sangre Road, thank you, too. **Sangre Road** came from my first summer in a rural Oklahoma college town that I christened with the name of a nearby ghost town. Sometimes, the people who are stuck in college towns after the spring semester stagnate during the dog days of summer, but those same folks will talk without speaking and tell a story I am forced to write down when watched closely. Enjoy.

Moses Kincaid will return soon.

DAVID TROMBLAY served in the U.S. Armed Forces for over a decade before attending the Institute of American Indian Arts for his MFA in Creative Writing. He is the author of *The Essentials: a Manifesto*, *As You Were: a Memoir*, and *The Ramblings of a Revenant*. He lives in Oklahoma with his cats, Walter and Winston; and his dogs, Bentley and Hank.

PREVIEW

David Tromblay

Money
the Hard
Way

COMING 2022

I

IT'S WEIRD—for lack of a better word—the number of fledgling couches and recliners that try to take flight from truck beds moving at expressway speeds. The downside is how, unlike Hippie Christmas, none of them are any good for the taking. There's no nursing them back to health, no matter how many popsicle sticks you use.

I've seen crews picking up crows off the shoulder using pitchforks in the past. But I couldn't imagine how many agencies play hot potato with the responsibility of cleaning up defunct furniture until it finally becomes part of the landscape, grows grass and other flora thanks to all the bird shit that gets splattered on it over the seasons. That's my roundabout way of saying my extended-stay room had a freeway-facing catwalk that dead-ended at my door, which I took to calling my front porch once I'd taken note of the motel tan I'd acquired. I'd taken on an olive-y hue from my overnight poolside tanning sessions beneath the neon saguaro cactus sign the hotel's proprietors hoisted over the pool. The pool looked green, whether it was between the hours of dusk and dawn or while the water was being warmed by the high-noon sun. If I were running things, I wouldn't bother with a NO LIFEGUARD ON DUTY sign. I'd post a DUCKS UNLIMITED sign along the fence and save a nice chunk of change on the chlorine I dare speculate they were happy to cut with tricycle motor piss.

The olive-y hue made me unrecognizable to myself in the silver-flecked bathroom mirror. The look grew on me once it hit me how maybe somebody might mistake me for an Italian or some other sort of Mediterranean-looking gentleman rather than a coydog who wandered off the reservation.

"Checking out today, Mr. Kink—aid?" the maid said, stuttering over a Freudian slip once her eyes caught sight of the handcuffs and other bondage restraints piled atop the chest of drawers next to the leaning tower of pizza boxes from The Pie Hole.

"Not that I am aware," I answered and knocked the half-empty bottle of Fentanyl and box of .45 ACP ammunition into the top drawer of the bedside table along with the good word from the Gideons and the old man's 1911 itself, all of which I hoped to hide from her prying eyes. "Towels, though, please," I said.

"I hope you're not leaving us," she said once more—not so much looking at me as trailing her eyes up the bedspread toward the hand that held the nightstand drawer closed while she distractedly set down a stack of clean towels on the foot of the bed. "You're so quiet of a man."

I could see the b-rated horror movie flicker behind her eyeballs with foreshadowed certainty she'd find me after I'd emptied the bottle and the contents of my intestinal tract onto the bedspread and down into the mattress, staining it so bad maintenance would have to drag it out to the dumpster. That or her having to sponge my dried brains and blood off the wallpaper and headboard with one part bleach and nine parts water, so they could rent the room again once it aired out.

She'd have to tip herself from whatever cash waited in my wallet, and she'd shit herself when she saw how much that was and didn't have to take the bus back and forth to work any longer. If she were smart, though, she would sign the title of the Mirada over to herself and take a little vacation away from work until she could shake the image of my bloated corpus. Her theory was plausible but had one glaring plot twist of a hole in it, however.

I'd fallen for Oklahoma.

Four months passed since another former soldier came down to Oklahoma from Kansas. That mother-fucker loaded a box truck down with forty bags of fer-tilizer, almost three hundred sticks of stolen water-gel explosives, and enough detonation cord to strangle the life out of one hundred and sixty-eight unsuspecting souls—nineteen of which were children. The nonstop updates of entered evidence and findings of the grand jury reported from outside the Perry courthouse proved more than I could take, so I took myself for a long romantic walk out into the tropical August afternoon.

On the far side of the interstate underpass, I spied with my little eye a business the size of a taco truck with the wheels taken off advertising notary and process ser-vice, private investigations, bail bonds. Some will go their entire life without as much as slowing their vehicle when they pass one; others come and go with such frequency they'd love it if revolving doors became standard in the construction like the gate at the city jail. Yet for me, the taqueria turned state-certified bail bond agent's office looked a lot like an employment agency, except with everything advertised in that lettering you'd swear they'd trademarked for Louis L'Amour's paperback novels.

The interior decorator didn't miss a single detail. Upon pulling open the glass door, my doing so got announced by a cowbell dangling overhead. Immediately after that, I had to push my way through a pair of swinging saloon doors. Next to the horseshoes for hat racks and spurs drilled into the wall for coat hooks, hung a mirror framed with what looked like a wanted poster from the old west. A cowhide rug carpeted the sitting area, and a bench upholstered with a knockoff Pendleton blanket sat snug against the wall, bookended by two matching wooden ma and pa rocking chairs. Centered above that were a mounted electric blue Mexican sombrero, a beaver felt ten-gallon hat, and a spray-painted aluminum trail's end silhouette still adorned with the HECHO EN MEXICO sticker. On the bond agent's desk sat a pair of horns stolen from the hood of Boss Hogg's Cadillac.

"Howdy, take a number, take a seat. I'll be one minute," came from behind the door with the hand-painted crescent moon and northern star, followed by a flush.

Scattered over the coffee table looked to be about two and a half–three years' worth of *Cowboys & Indians Magazine*.

"I'm guessing you're next," he said, slamming his back into the bathroom door to get it to latch all the way. He flared his nostrils and sucked in a sharp whiff into his chest, "Coffee's still hot," he said, looking off toward the back corner of the building. "I wouldn't say 'no' to a cup, too, if you're pouring one for yourself."

I poured him a cup, brought it over to his desk, and then went back for one of my own. He sat behind his desk and beneath the stuffed buffalo head mounted on the wall. From the far corner of the office, I could see how the buffalo wore a cavalry Stetson. The theme was coming together nicely. "God gave you two hands, why don't you use them?" he said, pointing his right hand at mine stuffed into the front pocket of my jeans.

"I was hoping to find a HELP WANTED sign in your window," I said.

At that, he scooted his chair back and slid open the center drawer on his desk, and his hand disappeared inside, "You're about as subtle as an auctioneer with Tourettes, now aren't you?" I was still processing his analogy when he elaborated in plainer language, "I'll be equally coy, what are you hiding in that hand you got stuck down inside your pocket there?"

I looked down at my right elbow and flopped it like a chicken wing, "I got into a car wreck a while back, and the sling got me too many questions from people I wasn't wanting to converse with."

"Makes sense," he said. "Pull up a chair." And I did, "You're not left-handed, huh?"

"No, I am not," I said, dragging the chair this way and then that.

"Work?" He mused, sounding skeptical. "There's always work that needs doing, but you can't be any geek off the street," he said, loosely quoting a pal of Billy Bonney.

I stayed quiet, let him talk, chewed on my coffee that somehow thickened as it cooled.

"I don't have applications for people to fill out," he said. "This work boils down to your resume. Let's start with your name."

"Moses Kincaid."

"Mmm…no, that sounds too starched. If I keep you around, I'll call you 'Kinky.'"

"Okay, and what do I call you, sir?"

"My name. Arlo Bice."

"Bice?"

"Yeah, Bice like *Miami Vice*—just with more bass."

"Okay, Mr. Bice."

"Arlo."

"Arlo then."

"Mister Arlo."

This Mister Arlo stood about six and a half feet tall—a whole head taller than me, at least—and Black as my shadow. The rodeo advert for the Bull-Dogger, Bill Pickett, and the *Buck and the Preacher* movie poster he'd framed, along with the Charlie Pride and Clarence "Gatemouth" Brown vinyl LP covers he'd tacked to the wall all said something so clearly there was no need for him to elaborate or reiterate a single word.

The comedy behind having an autographed photo of Leon "The Boogie Man," Coffee standing between the creamer and percolator did dawn on me after a while but looked out of place at first glance. Short of getting caught up on his nickname, it was hard to tell there was a Black man inside that barrel, beneath the cowboy hat and all that clown makeup.

The long-sleeved, embroidered western shirt Mister Arlo wore cinched at the neck with a braided-leather bolo tie, tucked into his double-stitched, slim-fit Wranglers held up by a buckle commemorating the eightieth anniversary of the Oklahoma State Penitentiary Rodeo sent home the message how there are rednecks and hillbillies and coonasses, but then there are Okies who should never be confused with any of the aforementioned.

"Were, about the same age, I'm guessing," he said, "I'm messing about the Mister Arlo thing. Don't disrespect me, and I'll do the same."

"Can I call you 'Tubbs?'"

"You can view now as the appropriate time to dazzle me with your resume."

"Former Army—"

"Calvary?" he said as he cut me off and stretched his pointer finger toward the taxidermy mount on the wall above his head.

"Nope. Custer had enough scouts."

"Oh, Indian, huh? Wasn't all that sure."

"I was an MP, deployed to Haiti for a while, spent some time at Leavenworth, Kans—"

"Which side of the bars?"

"Outside."

"Mmm, okay. What else?" Arlo said, looking bored, but bound to find something successfully eluding him in one of his desk drawers.

"Worked around Kansas City, collecting bail jumpers after that."

"Finally," he said, looking up from his desk drawer. Arlo took the time to lock eyes with me before he smiled and added, "Some relevant work experience."

I didn't want him to know that was it, so I stayed quiet like I was being polite and waiting for him to add something else to his appraisal of my CV.

"Haiti was last year, wasn't it?" He said, searching the wall behind me for the calendar.

"It was," I answered. "Got out a little before last Halloween."

"It's only August, so you've been at this for less than a year?"

"A little over six months," I said, already seeing where things were headed.

"So, you're not green, but you are not yellow, either, now are you?"

Again, I let him talk, squared my jar for some dumbass reason, like when a woman wraps her arm around yours, and you flex your bicep to try to impress her.

"You're not going to pad your resume, tell me how you were a Ranger or Special Forces or any other kind of Billy Badass?"

"Nope," I said. "I am what I am."

He smiled at that, wet his lips, and said, "You're a brokedick Popeye wanting to work as a bounty hunter? For me?"

"Time heals all wounds," I said, not wanting the interview to be over because of a bum shoulder. "And freelance is fine. Private contractor, or however you want to phrase it."

"No, that won't be an allowable condition of your employment, Kinky. See, as an employer, I am a lot like a jealous girlfriend—I won't share my men with anyone."

"That's fair. As long as work is steady."

"That it is. Now, if we're done feeling each other up, I think we know who is pitching and who is catching," Arlo said and paused to clear his throat while closing the desk drawer. "Some guy put his Viper up as collateral. I did not think that ding-dong would let his trial date come and go without showing his face, but that is why business is plentiful."

"Okay."

"I'm going to give you an address," he said, peeling a post-it away from the pad and handing it across the desk. I pocketed the paper and looked up in time to see him toss a key at my head.

"What's this for?" I asked, running my thumb over the black plastic snake's hissing mouth.

"Fetch."

BOOKS

On the following pages are a few
more great titles from the
Down & Out Books publishing family.
For a complete list of books and to
sign up for our newsletter,
go to **DownAndOutBooks.com**.

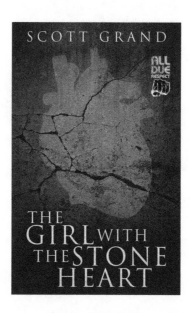

The Girl with the Stone Heart
Scott Grand

All Due Respect, an imprint of
Down & Out Books
November 2020
978-1-64396-122-4

Winter has set in a small town on the California coast and a fishing vessel has been lost amongst the gray waves. Grace runs the bowling alley and ghosts through his own life. He lives in the layer of fat between the underbelly and society.

Grace is charged with issuing payments to the fishermen's widows. He pulls on his funeral suit and borrows his grandmother's New Yorker. When Grace is unable to find one woman, he uncovers something that threatens the oligarchy's reign and his way of life.

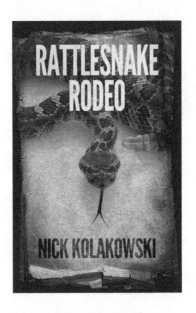

Rattlesnake Rodeo
A Boise Longpig Hunting Club Thriller
Nick Kolakowski

Down & Out Books
October 2020
978-1-64396-128-6

The fiery sequel to *Boise Longpig Hunting Club* is here...

Jake Halligan and his ultra-lethal sister Frankie have survived the Boise Longpig Hunting Club. What comes next, though, might prove far worse.

With the law closing in, they'll have to make the hardest choices if they want to survive.

Chasing China White
Allan Leverone

Shotgun Honey, an imprint of
Down & Out Books
September 2019
978-1-64396-029-6

When heroin junkie Derek Weaver runs up an insurmountable debt with his dealer, he's forced to commit a home invasion to wipe the slate clean.

Things go sideways and Derek soon finds himself a multiple murderer in the middle of a hostage situation.

With seemingly no way out, he may discover the key to redemption lies in facing down long-ignored demons.

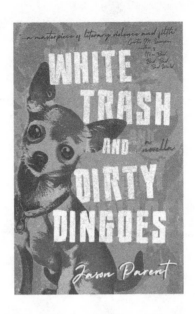

White Trash and Dirty Dingoes
Jason Parent

Shotgun Honey, an imprint of
Down & Out Books
July 2020
978-1-64396-101-9

Gordon thought he'd found the girl of his dreams. But women like Sarah are tough to hang on to.

When she causes the disappearance of a mob boss's priceless Chihuahua, she disappears herself, and the odds Gordon will see his lover again shrivel like nuts in a polar plunge.

With both money and love lost, he's going to have to kill some SOBs to get them back.

CPSIA information can be obtained
at www.ICGtesting.com
Printed in the USA
LVHW091659200621
690709LV00006B/1049